MORGAN: FIREBRAND COWBOYS

BARB HAN

TORJAKE PUBLISHING

Copyright © 2023 by Barb Han

All rights reserved.

No part of this book may be reproduced in any form or by any electronic or mechanical means, including information storage and retrieval systems, without written permission from the author, except for the use of brief quotations in a book review.

Editing: Ali Williams

Cover Design: Jacob's Cover Designs

To Brandon, Jacob, and Tori for being the great loves of my life. To Babe for being my place to call home.

1

Who the hell was knocking at this late hour?

Nine forty-five wasn't late by most folks' standards, but ranchers started their day at four o'clock in the morning. It was long past time to go to bed. Morgan had been restless lately, thinking too much about his mother sitting in jail. Lost on how she could have spiraled so far.

He shelved those unproductive thoughts as he opened the door.

"Good evening, Sheriff Lawler," Morgan said, more than a little concerned at the house call.

The two exchanged greetings and a handshake. Timothy Lawler had been two grades ahead of his cousin Adam in school, so they knew of each other. Lawler had been a star quarterback who was being scouted by some big-name programs when he took a hit that broke his arm in four places. He'd managed to get off the game-winning throw, but the injury had ended his career and any hopes of playing college ball. He'd gone to school and studied criminal justice instead and then followed in his father's footsteps in law enforcement. The man was about as fair-skinned as they came. He had ginger hair in a military cut, a hawk-like nose, and compassionate honey-brown eyes. He wore jeans, boots, and a tan shirt with the word, Sheriff, embroidered on the right front pocket.

"What can I do for you?" Morgan asked, his blood pressure rising.

"I have a few questions for you," Lawler said, giving away nothing with his expression. The man was all business. "May I come inside?"

Morgan opened the door wider with a nod. The sheriff followed him into the kitchen area of Morgan's log cabin style home. It had two bedrooms, a living room that was open to the dining room, and a small galley kitchen. The place was all Morgan needed to be comfortable after a long day working cattle.

"I'll get straight to the point," Lawler said in a tone that matched his tense expression.

Morgan stood at the granite island as he folded his arms across his chest. "Alright. What can I do for you?"

"I have questions about the dates you've been on from DateApp," Lawler said. "I apologize for the personal nature of the line of questioning, but it's relevant to a case or I wouldn't be here."

It went without saying, but Morgan played along. He threw his hands in the air. "I'm afraid I don't know anything about such an app. And the last date I went on was..." He stopped to think about it when the answer didn't immediately come to him. He'd been too busy or, more realistically, too bored with what felt like Groundhog Day of dates to go out much recently. "I guess it's been a minute." He brought his hand up to scratch his head. "I'd say four months, give or take."

The sheriff's left eyebrow flew up. "Are you certain about that?"

"Do you have evidence to the contrary?" Morgan asked, getting right to the point. There was no use beating around the bush.

"I have an IP address and your profile," Lawler informed, pulling out his cell. He tapped the screen a few times and then tilted the device toward Morgan so he could see.

Morgan took a step closer. "That's my picture and it's definitely my name, but I promise you right here and now that I have no idea about the dating site. This is the first I've seen or heard of it."

Lawler studied Morgan for a long moment. The sheriff must be deciding if he believed him or not.

"What else does it say? Is there some other information in the profile?" Morgan asked, wanting to know just how much the imposter knew about him and his life.

The sheriff scrolled.

A few words stuck out as Morgan skimmed the text. *Cattle rancher.* He couldn't deny that one. *Single.* That was true. *Looking for love.* Definitely not. He pointed toward the phrase. "I would never say something like that, let alone write it for the world to see."

Lawler nodded.

"It's a lie," he defended. "But I'm guessing you'll need more proof than my word."

"The profile alone isn't as incriminating at the IP address," Lawler admitted. "In fact, if it wasn't for that, I wouldn't even be here." He paused. "Folks have been known to set up fake profiles before."

"Let's say, for the sake of argument, that I'm innocent here," Morgan stated. "I am, by the way. But why would I set this up? Last I checked, it's not illegal to set up a profile on one of these dating apps."

"It is when the last person you corresponded with on the app ends up missing," Lawler pointed out.

Morgan bit back a curse. A female responded to the fake profile and was now nowhere to be found. Would the sheriff assume Morgan was involved just because of his mother's recent attempted murder charge? Did everyone look guilty now?

He put his hands up, palms out in the surrender position. "Do I need an attorney present for the rest of this conversation?"

"That would be entirely up to you," Lawler said. "I have no intention of placing you under arrest this evening, if that helps sway your decision."

The words, *this evening,* weren't exactly reassuring.

"I'll hold off for now," Morgan said after a thoughtful pause. "But I have to ask. Is there any chance this can be tied to my mother's case?"

"I can tell you that a young lady filed a missing person report in Austin. It came to my attention when a citizen of my county came into question as part of the investigation," Lawler informed. "I'm answering a call for cooperation from Austin PD and said I'd check the situation out on my end." He shrugged. "My guess is that if Austin believed the claimant, they would have assigned a detective to the case. This came across my desk as a request for professional courtesy."

"Meaning, if you check me out and give the all clear, they'll drop it," Morgan surmised.

"That's the idea," Lawler said. "Or, at the very least, they'll bark up another tree. They've already called hospitals and jails. The risk assessment in Austin is low."

"Meaning?"

"She isn't deemed likely to hurt herself," Lawler said. "She isn't wanted for a crime, so there's no legal ramifications for going missing."

"I might be asking the obvious here," Morgan continued, "but is it possible the person in question decided to go off the grid of her own free will? Or is in a location where cell connection isn't possible?"

Lawler nodded. "There's a concerned party who believes otherwise. Law enforcement does its best to locate the individual in question when a worried citizen brings a missing person to our attention."

"I'm guessing whoever created the fake profile page of me was recently in contact with this person," Morgan said.

"That's correct," Lawler confirmed.

Morgan issued a sharp sigh. "I don't know what to tell you about the profile, except that I had no hand in creating it. You're welcome to check my laptop."

"I'd appreciate having a look," Lawler said.

"Check my phone while you're at it." Morgan retrieved both and set them on top of the granite island in the kitchen area. He booted up his laptop and scrolled through apps on his phone. "In my line of work, I don't have cell coverage most of my working day, so I use this thing for texts and phone calls when I'm in range."

"I'm not seeing the dating app," Lawler confirmed.

"You won't find it on my laptop either," Morgan continued as he gave the sheriff access.

After a minute of searching, Lawler shook his head. "Not finding anything there either."

"And you won't because I've never signed up for a dating app," Morgan said. "But I plan to get to the bottom of how someone used my picture to set one up. Don't these apps have a responsibility to verify a user's identity?"

"They're all different," Lawler replied. "Some go deeper than others. Whoever set your profile up was tech savvy enough to use your IP. I'll let you know if I have any additional questions," he continued after making a few notes on his cell phone. "I appreciate your cooperation."

Morgan showed the sheriff out and then closed and locked the door behind him. There was a time in Lone Star Pass when he wouldn't have thought twice about leaving his home unlocked or keys in the truck. Times were changing and it was better to be safe than sorry.

Gravel crunched underneath tires as the sheriff pulled away. Morgan cut off the kitchen light and then headed toward the bedroom, hoping it didn't take too long for the missing person to turn up. He probably should have asked for more details in the case so he could dig around. Although, he doubted the sheriff would volunteer the information.

He brushed his teeth, washed up, and then stripped down to boxer shorts for sleeping. Sitting on the side of his bed, he grabbed his cell and skimmed the news to see if anything had been written about fake dating profiles turning up. It unnerved him that someone had used his name and likeness to set up an account. He pulled up the site, figuring he needed to shoot a message to their customer service department to flag the profile as a fake.

As he finished up the message, a noise sounded outside. Morgan knew the layout of his cabin by heart, so he didn't need to turn on the light to walk around. Instead, he palmed his cell phone and dimmed the brightness to next to nothing.

The noise came from around the back of the cabin. A

fleeting thought the sheriff might be coming back to snoop around tried to take hold. Morgan dismissed it. Lawler had been honest and upfront. Plus, he hadn't been invited to hang around.

Morgan grabbed his shotgun from the coat closet near the front door and loaded a shell. He slipped out the front door and then made his way around the side of the cabin, heading the long way where it was dark.

With his back against the outside of his cabin, he turned the corner to find a female figure bent over his trash can, digging around. What the hell?

"Stop right there and put your hands where I can see 'em," he demanded, lifting the shotgun so the barrel pointed right at the center of the woman as he stepped into the light.

AVRIL CAPRI BROUGHT her hand up to cover a gasp. She quickly lifted both in the air, following the imposing man's command before he fired. "Stop. Please. Don't shoot. Are you Morgan Firebrand?"

His profile said he was six-feet-three-inches and spent most of his days working cattle. In person, his physical size was more intimidating than she expected. As he stepped into the light, she realized he had on nothing but boxers. Assessing the threat level caused her to take in his tall, muscled frame. He had big hands—hands that could probably crush her skull if he wanted to. He was stealth. And he was quick.

Did he have her sister Mazie?

"What the hell are you doing here and why do you know

my name?" he asked, staring at her from behind the barrel of a shotgun.

"I'm looking for my sister," she stated, trying to level her now jacked-up pulse. Her voice shook with fear and her mouth dried up.

"In the trash?"

"No," she quicky countered. Then, realized how this must look. Folks in these parts had a right to shoot trespassers if they came across as a threat. She prayed the rancher would hold off until she could explain. "I'm sorry for coming here unannounced, but my sister is missing and I thought—"

The man cut her off with his glare.

"I'm desperate," she pleaded, regaining her voice. "Please don't shoot."

Thankfully, he lowered the weapon. The light cast shadows on a face etched from granite. From this distance, she couldn't see his eyes clearly or read his intentions. But he dropped the business end of the weapon toward the ground.

"Why are you digging around in my trash?" he asked. His strong, masculine voice was a study in calm. Deep and gravelly, it caused her arms to goosebump and her body to ache with something that felt a lot like need. She chalked it up to fear, not desire.

"Like I said, I'm trying to find my sister," she admitted.

"You must be the concerned citizen the sheriff mentioned," he half mumbled, barely loud enough for her to hear.

"I'll just be on my way," she said, hoping it would be that easy to walk away. Her car was parked on the side of the road a mile away. Coming here unannounced had been the worst of bad ideas and screamed of her desperation. As a self-defense teacher, she should have known better.

"Not so fast," he warned, keeping the barrel lowered as he walked toward her. "Come inside where we can talk."

She shook her head. "That's not a good idea."

He softened his stance. "You want information about me and I have questions of my own. Seems to me the quickest way for both of us to get what we want is to head inside and have a conversation."

Could she trust the man? At this point, did she have a choice?

"My name is Morgan Firebrand, like you asked," he said as he stopped a foot in front of her. He offered his hand, balancing the shotgun in the crook of his arm.

She took the firm handshake. "Avril Capri."

"Sheriff Lawler was here a little while ago," he said. "He checked my cell and my laptop to see if I set up the dating app profile that your sister may have been using before she disappeared." He paused for a few seconds. "I didn't. Getting to the bottom of who did and why is understandably more important to you. But now that my name is involved, I plan to see the investigation through. You're welcome to call the sheriff to verify that everything I just said is true. You could tell him that you stopped by if you're worried about being alone with me." He glanced at the log cabin. "I live alone, so there's no one else inside."

The rancher walked away before she could respond. He was right. She had questions. She'd been naïve enough to believe she could slip onto his property and dig around without getting caught. It was time to face the music. Her sister Mazie's life might depend on the information this man could provide, so she followed him.

Stopping on the porch, she pulled out her cell and sent

her neighbor a text message that she was walking inside Morgan Firebrand's cabin. That way, if she didn't come out again there would be a record. Instincts said she could trust him, but she needed proof and a failsafe.

"Give me a minute to throw on some clothes," Morgan said after flipping on the light and leaving the front door open.

"Okay," Avril said, palming her phone as she stepped inside the unfamiliar place. She closed the door behind her but stood right next to it, her hand at the ready. If she needed to grip the handle, it would take very little movement. She glanced around the room in search of anything that could be used as a makeshift weapon.

Her heart pounded against her ribcage, beating erratically. *Deep breaths.*

Morgan returned, wearing jeans and a black t-shirt that only highlighted a body that was obviously used for hard labor and rigorous workouts. Honest blue eyes with the thickest black eyelashes looked right at her. *Through her?*

"If you're uncomfortable, we can leave the door open," Morgan said. "But I can't promise insects won't bombard us."

He took a seat on a leather chair in the living room and then motioned toward the couch.

Avril walked a couple of steps and then sat down. She'd already cased the place and decided this was the home of a normal person. It was tidy and the decorations were sparse, but there was something calming about the décor and the simplicity of the space.

"Tell me about your sister," Morgan said, clasping his hands as he leaned forward.

2

Being looked at as a possible kidnapper wasn't exactly on Morgan's list of life goals. But one look at Avril's desperation softened his frustration at the situation. If one of his siblings disappeared, he would move heaven and earth to find them. He couldn't fault her for digging through his trash when he might have gone to similar lengths if he thought he had a real lead.

"Mazie is her name. She's my younger sister by ten years," Avril began, holding onto her phone so tightly that her knuckles turned white. She shook her head and shrugged. "She's always been the free-spirited one between the two of us, but this has obviously gone too far. She's never gone this far without making contact."

Avril tucked a piece of thick, dark hair behind her ear. Her hair had a reddish tint. The color looked almost burgundy. Her big beautiful eyes were an intense shade of blue. It was almost like looking into another world.

Otherwise, she had an oval face and full soft, kissable pink lips. Her closed-off demeanor gave the impression she was a serious individual, and that few people got past the walls she clearly had up now despite the circumstances.

"What makes you think your sister Mazie didn't decide to take time off from life?" he asked.

"She wouldn't do that without sending a text first," Avril defended, but it was clear he'd struck a chord when she tensed up.

"Did she always let you know where she was going to be and when?" he asked. He'd dated a true free spirit once. She would disappear for a couple of days before suddenly popping back into his phone.

"No," she said with almost brutal honesty. "But she wouldn't just disappear on me like this."

"How do you know?" he asked.

"I just do," she said defensively.

He wasn't trying to rile her up.

"I'm just asking because I had the sheriff stop by a little while ago, asking me questions about a profile that I never set up," he said, once again getting right to the point. This wasn't exactly the time to be coy. A life could possibly be on the line, and he risked jail time if he didn't clear his name. "So, I'm afraid that I'm behind the eight ball on this one."

"Welcome to the club," she said on a frustrated sigh.

"Let's be honest with each other then," he said. "I have no idea why someone chose my name to hide behind, but I don't take it lightly."

Another sigh deflated her chest. It was probably easier to believe he was involved. Now that she heard he wasn't, she would have to start over. As much as he could sympathize, Morgan didn't love the idea he was being cast in the light of a possible abductor or worse. His mother's actions had placed a dark cloud over the family. Was it one that had made the sheriff drop by unannounced rather than call or text?

The way Avril sat perched on the chair closest to the door reminded him that she was in his home, despite being afraid. He might not have been thrilled to find someone going through his trash, but he was even less psyched about her being scared of him.

"And I'd also like to point out that you're the one trespassing on my land and I have a right to call the sheriff," he continued. "But then you'd be the one behind bars and I can't have that while you're trying to find your sister."

"Don't tell me you suddenly care about my well-being," she said with a look.

He put a hand up. "I didn't mean to come off like I didn't care. Of course, I do. Ranchers live by a code that says we help each other out."

She conceded with a nod.

"Since Austin PD is involved, I'm guessing that's where your sister lives," he said.

"Yes," she confirmed. "Downtown." Avril tightened her grip on the cell. The woman would be considered beautiful by most standards with her thick auburn hair that fell past her shoulders. Those shrewd blue eyes seemed like she could look right through a person. How could her sister get one over on someone like Avril? She responded with as few words as possible, so not the talkative type. Though, it could have more to do with the circumstances than anything else.

"I have to ask, so pardon the bluntness of the next question," he said.

Avril's lips compressed into a frown and her gaze dropped to the wood flooring like making eye contact would somehow make this worse.

"Are we looking for a body?" he asked as gently as he could.

She squeezed her eyes shut as she shook her head. "No. At least, not yet."

"Then, we're looking for someone who is still alive," he said, thinking out loud.

"That's the hope," she continued.

"Which is why this search has even more urgency," he deduced.

"If I have a chance to find my sister alive, I'm going to take it if that's what you're saying," she said. "The longer she's gone, the worse her chances are based on everything I've read."

"We both want the same thing," he reassured. "So, tell me more about Mazie so we can find her."

"I thought all you wanted was to clear your own name," she said, looking caught off guard.

"If I can help find her, it's my responsibility," he said before leaning forward, resting his elbows on his knees. "Now that I've met you, I'm even more determined."

If those words meant anything to Avril, she didn't give her reaction away. In fact, she'd make an amazing poker player.

"I appreciate your..." she flashed eyes at him, "...*interest* in my sister's disappearance, but I work best alone."

"Working together will help us cover more ground," he pointed out.

Her forehead creased as she contemplated those words.

"Tell me more about your sister," he said, capitalizing on the non-rejection. Plus, the more he knew about Mazie, the better chance he had of figuring out what might make her disappear other than the obvious answer of being abducted. "What does she do for a living?"

"Mazie runs a video channel with a loyal following," Avril said. "It's another reason why I know she wouldn't just disappear. She posts every Monday, Wednesday, and Friday." She heaved a sigh and toyed with the phone in her hand. "Until two weeks ago."

Fourteen days was a long time for someone to be missing.

"Is that when you realized she might be MIA?" he asked.

Avril shook her head. "I called in the missing person report nine days ago, but Austin considered the threat low because the last couple of videos my sister put up hinted at a surprise coming."

Basically, it took her five days to realize her sister was missing. Hadn't he read something about the first twenty-four hours or so being critical?

"I'm guessing there are no other concerned parties in this case and that you have no idea what surprise she was talking about," he recapped.

"My sister only recently started dating someone, but I have no idea who he is since it's not you," she admitted. "What else did the sheriff say?"

"Not a whole lot," Morgan admitted. "All he wanted to do was get a statement from me and my cooperation, which I gave. I already told you about him checking my devices. I'm happy to show you the same."

"It's fine," she said. "I believe you."

That was progress. He'd take it.

"He did say the person he's looking for will have decent computer skills," Morgan continued. "The person has the profile linked to my IP address."

"My sister has a tech guy she works with when she needs help with her channel or has general computing or equipment questions," Avril offered.

Now, they might be getting somewhere.

"Have you met this person?" he asked.

She shook her head. "Mazie talked to me about her life and work, but she did her own thing. We were lucky to meet up for coffee as often as we did."

"It's easy to take family for granted," he said, wanting to add *until it's too late*. He had regrets about his own. Case in point, he would always feel guilty about not noticing how far his mother had spiraled. He would always question whether or not any of them could have stopped her before she'd attempted murder. Speaking of Jackie Firebrand, he needed to visit her in jail, except that he couldn't think of one thing to say to her. The two had never been close. Even at a young age, he'd spotted her gold-digger tendencies. Considering she'd never been the 'mothering' type, he'd cut bait early on their relationship. Now? He wished he could go back and somehow stop her from hitting rock bottom. Money to her was like drugs to an addict.

Morgan gave a mental headshake. This wasn't the time to think about his family. He refocused on Avril, who was studying him as she snapped her fingers, like she was trying to bring him back from a trance.

Her eyebrow arched. "Are you okay?"

She had no idea how loaded the question was. Or did she?

"What do you know about my family?"

"The quick answer is that I ran an internet search before I came here tonight," Avril said, almost hating to admit it now that she saw the disappointment on his face. "I was coming here alone. Unarmed." Except for the Swiss Army knife in her purse, that she currently had a grip around with her free hand. With her handbag flat on her lap, it had been easy to slip her hand inside and locate the weapon.

"It makes sense to take precautions," he said with a hint of something that sounded a lot like shame in his voice. "You know about my family's *situation*."

"Yes, I do," she admitted.

"You said that you aren't carrying," he said.

"That's right."

"Do you mind telling me why you have your hand inside your purse?" he asked, folding his arms across a broad chest.

She pulled out the knife. "This is supposed to be insurance."

"I can walk you to your vehicle if you'd like," he said, sounding defensive.

"Are you asking me to leave?"

"No," he said. "It catches me off guard that someone could be afraid of me, and I thought you might want to resume discussion tomorrow in a public place."

"Oh," she said. His response was reasonable. "I didn't know anything about you or your family before all this."

"I don't blame you for showing up here," he conceded. "Hell, I might do the same if I was in your boots. But I don't want you to be uncomfortable with me, and being in public is the only way I know how to accomplish that. Not to mention, you've clamped down on a yawn several times in the last few minutes. I'm guessing you're more tired than you'd like to admit to yourself."

"I am," she said, "but—"

"We can continue this discussion in the morning," he interrupted with a look of sympathy. "Early."

Avril dropped the knife inside her handbag and stood. She knew when she'd lost a battle. And, truth be told, she was tired. So very tired. It had been nine days since she'd had a good night of sleep.

"Where are you parked?" he asked as he stood up.

"About a mile from here on the side of the road," she said. "How did you know I parked somewhere else?"

"The sheriff's vehicle were the only tires I heard," he said by way of explanation.

"Of course," she remarked.

"You traipsed through the woods to get here because that's the only way," he said. "I figured as much when I found you digging through my trash."

When he put it like that, she did come across as the unbalanced one between the two of them. "I appreciate you for not calling the sheriff to report me for trespassing."

He nodded. "I can't judge too harshly when I might have done the same."

"Somehow, I doubt it," she stated, walking toward the door. "I apologize for—"

"Don't," he cut her off. "You're trying to find your sister. You don't need to say another word." He paused. "Believe it or not, we're on the same team here."

Was that even possible? The thought of having someone else to lean on was almost too good to be true.

Avril shelved the thought. It *was* too good to be true. She'd been taking care of herself and her sister long enough to prove it. Although to be fair, Mazie resisted any attempts to be taken care of once she turned seventeen and could legally drop out of school.

The string of foster parents she'd been assigned to had been in it for the money, not following a calling to help children no one wanted or could care for. Mazie had been bounced around one too many times in Avril's book. Not being able to protect her sister had been the greatest failure of her life. But that was a long time ago. What happened in childhood wasn't anyone's fault. Bringing those same wounds into adulthood was a whole different story. That felt more like a choice and Avril chose to move on.

The mile walk went by faster than Avril remembered. Then again, going to someplace always seemed to take longer than coming back. She'd observed it on road trips over the years. Road trips that had her chasing down leads that left her hoping she'd finally found her and Mazie's father. The man had been a bust. He was one of those people who'd peaked early in life.

She realized on the trail that the rancher was going to have to make this walk twice, which also told her that he was a decent person. She highly doubted anyone would go out of their way as much as him to ensure she felt safe. Hell, he'd been the one to suggest she leave to get some rest. Not exactly the actions of someone who wanted to abduct her, harm her, or worse.

Besides, wouldn't he have done so already?

"Thank you for seeing me to my car safely," she said as they approached the sedan.

He waved her off like the gesture was nothing. To her, it meant the world. It also gave her confidence in extending trust. She could only pray she wouldn't regret the decision.

"Where are you staying?" he asked before heading back.

"Motel on the highway," she answered. "It's nothing, just close."

"Mind if we exchange numbers so you can let me know you safely arrived?" he asked. His concern for her well-being brought on a stab of guilt she'd so easily categorized him as a potential monster after reading up on his family. The old saying, *like mother like son*, had come to mind after learning of his mother's incarceration.

When had she become so quick to judge? If someone took a hard look at her family, they'd find the cracks. Hell, it wouldn't even have to be hard. All they'd have to do would be ask a few questions to learn her father had disappeared early on, apparently not thinking two daughters and a wife were enough to stick around for. And then her mother had worked two jobs to keep food on the table until she was gone too. A diagnosis in November followed by a funeral in February when Mazie was ten years old and Avril was twenty. A severe flu outbreak had been the cause, which had brought on pneumonia. Her mother's weakened immune system couldn't take the hit. She'd hid her lupus diagnosis for years prior, not wanting her girls to worry.

If Avril had known what was going to happen, she would have done things differently. She would have insisted on taking her mother out for lunch more and would have brought dinners over. She couldn't count the number of times her mother had asked for a Friday night movie night with her girls cuddling on the sofa. Busy with community college for nursing school and work, Avril had taken a pass too many times.

"Sure," she finally said, offering her cell.

When she glanced up, she realized Morgan was staring at her. Studying her?

"Sorry, I just had a flashback about my family," she said by way of explanation. After extending kindness to make sure she made it to her car safely, she felt she owed him a little bit of honesty. She held out her phone.

He nodded, and then took the offering.

"Here you go," he said after inputting his contact information. "I've sent a text, so you'll have my number."

Avril thanked him before slipping into the driver's seat and driving into the night. She blinked dry eyes as she drove down the country road full of potholes. Without streetlights, it was hard to see. While flipping on high beams, she nailed a pothole that caused her seatbelt to lock as she bounced. This seemed like a good time to pray her suspension held up.

After what felt like an eternity, she was on the service road leading toward the motel. All she had to do was hop on the highway for ten minutes and then she'd essentially be at the motel.

There weren't many vehicles on the road this evening, so when a truck came barreling up from behind her, she took note.

Avril changed lanes to get out of the jerk's way. His headlights were on high beams, which reminded her to dim hers. The truck immediately switched lanes, staying behind her. She would honk or flip them off but figured it wouldn't do any good. The person behind the wheel might be drunk.

She watched out the rearview after flipping to night view to escape the near-blinding headlights. She sped up. So did the driver behind her. She slowed down. So did he.

Her exit would be coming up soon, which was her only saving grace. Avril clamped down on the panic rising in her chest. Out here where there weren't other vehicles on this side of the highway freaked her out. A wreck could go unnoticed until it was too late to save anyone.

As she glanced at the sideview mirror, the truck rammed her bumper, causing her to spin out of control.

3

Morgan's cell buzzed on the nightstand. He snatched it, unable to sleep anyway. His mind had been spinning ever since talking to his surprise visitors. He checked the screen, wondering what else could go wrong tonight.

Avril?

"Hello?" he immediately answered.

"Help," she said, out of breath like she'd just sprinted across a football field.

"Where are you?" he asked, hopping up and into the pair of jeans he'd draped across the chair next to his bed. He stumbled with his phone to his ear, regained his balance, and then toed on his boots.

"At the exit to the motel where I'm staying," she said through labored breaths. "I've been hit."

"Did you call 911?" he asked.

"Yes," she said. "The closest emergency vehicle is forty-five minutes away."

"I'm thirty," he half-mumbled. "A little more than twenty if I fly."

"Be careful," she warned. "He might still be—"

The call dropped, and Morgan cursed the timing. Who the hell was *he*?

Morgan threw on a shirt and tried to call back with no luck. Cell phone service was spotty out here at the cabin. There was no telling how many times she'd tried to call him before it went through.

Within minutes, he was in his vehicle and zipping down the small country lane that led to the back exit of the property. If he'd known where her car had been parked earlier, he would have just driven her over. But Avril was new to these parts and didn't know east from west when it came to the family property. He knew the backroads like the back of his hand. Thirty-five years of life, all spent living on Firebrand land had taught him a thing or two about the terrain.

Getting a hold of Avril again proved impossible as his engine screamed down the road. He turned the steering wheel left to right and back as he navigated around potholes. One of the benefits of having a home here was that he knew those too.

His panic levels were hitting a high note by the time he drove up and stopped beside her dented and crunched up car. A truck was pulled ahead of hers with its flashers on. From the looks of it, she'd been hit hard.

Morgan pulled over, put the gearshift in park, and then bolted out of the driver's seat. He didn't bother turning off his engine.

The driver's side door was open and Avril sat sidesaddle in the seat, airbag flattened after it had deployed. Her gaze flew to him as he came running.

A young family flanked her. The woman cradled a baby in her arms and gently bounced the blue bundle.

"Morgan," Avril said as she met him halfway. "Thank you so

much for coming. I didn't know who else to call when the dispatcher asked for contact information for a family member."

"I'm glad you reached out," he said, relieved to see her walking on her own. His mind had envisioned a whole lot of scenarios on the way over. Every single one brought his stress levels up another few notches. "Are you injured?"

He scanned her for signs.

She glanced up and down her body. "I think I'm fine."

After the accident, she could be in shock. "I'd feel better if you sat down."

Avril leaned into him, so he looped his arms around her. She buried her face in his chest. He heard a few sniffles but when she looked up at him a few seconds later, her red-rimmed eyes were dry.

"What happened?" he asked as the couple with the new baby joined them.

"It looks like everything is under control here," the young man, who looked to be in his mid-twenties, said. He wore a wedding band on the hand he gripped his keys with. "Unless you need us to stay to give a statement, we need to get back on the road."

"Please, go," Avril said. "Thank you for stopping in the first place."

"We couldn't drive past and leave you on your own," the man said. His wife had black hair twisted in a pair of braids. The baby in her arms started fidgeting.

"Mind if we get your contact information in case the sheriff needs to corroborate the story?" Morgan asked.

"Not a problem," the young man said.

Morgan handed over his cell so he could input his information. When he was done, he handed the phone back. "Thank you."

The guy, Jose, nodded. He and his wife walked to their truck after wishing Avril well.

"This huge truck came up on my bumper," Avril said. "He slammed into me, which caused me to spin out. I heard crunches, but he sped away when Jose and his wife showed up. If they hadn't been driving down the road when they were..."

She shook her head.

"Not a drunk driver?" he asked, thinking it was possible this time of night.

"He didn't swerve, except to follow me every time I tried to get out of his way," she said. "He stayed on my backside and was aggressive. I highly doubt alcohol was involved, although he's gone now, so we can't test him."

"I'm relieved you're alright," Morgan admitted. "It's my fault this happened. I never should have let you leave."

The sound of sirens split the air.

"That's probably the law," she said, looking up at him with those blue orbs. "Is there any way we can skip the part about me trespassing on your land to root through your garbage as the reason I'm here?"

"I'm guessing the sheriff won't appreciate you for taking matters into your own hands," he said.

She shook her head. "I've already been warned."

It sounded like there was a story in the admission.

"Being Lawler was at my house earlier," he said. "It'll be suspicious if we don't tell him something believable. What are the odds the two of us would know each other?"

She took a step away from him and he missed her warmth against his skin in the chilly night air.

The truck with the family's taillights disappeared into the dark as the first peek of headlights, along with spinning emergency lights appeared in the opposite direction, coming their way. Avril folded her arms over her chest.

"You know what? Never mind," she said with a look of disdain. "I just asked you to lie to a law enforcement officer, which is illegal and could land you in trouble. That wasn't right. I'm not in my right mind since Mazie's disappearance." She shook her head. "Forget I said anything, okay? Be honest because it's the right thing to do and you could perjure yourself."

Morgan wanted to tell her that he understood her desperation, but he wasn't living in her circumstances. His protective instincts kicked into high gear, though. And he wanted to find a way to cover for her and still be honest. "I'll figure out something."

The sheriff would be looking into his phone records if he hadn't already. So, lying about knowing each other or the fact she'd reached out to him in advance wasn't an option. That would only make things worse for her.

Sheriff Lawler parked his SUV. An ambulance pulled up right behind him, along with a tow truck. He walked toward them with a raised eyebrow.

They had some explaining to do.

"Dispatch said Ms. Capri was involved in an accident," Lawler began.

"That's right," Avril said. "I'm the one who called in after one of those trucks with the huge tires ran me off the road. He stopped briefly, but he must have been spooked by another vehicle that came up on the road shortly after."

"Do you know what color the vehicle in question was?" Lawler asked. He asked other routine-sounding questions, asking after the make and model of the vehicle along with whether she got a description of the driver.

Details were sparse, giving the sheriff very little to go on.

A pair of EMTs interrupted. "I'd like permission to check the crash victim's vitals, Sheriff."

Lawler nodded.

"I'm Vic," the EMT said to Avril. "Follow me this way."

She walked over to the ambulance with the first responder.

"I have to say that I'm surprised to see you here," Sheriff Lawler said. "I had no idea you knew Ms. Capri."

"I didn't before this evening," Morgan admitted. "In truth, she stopped by not long after you did to ask a few questions, which I obliged."

The sheriff's face twisted in frustration. "She shouldn't have followed me to your home."

"How do you know she didn't find me on her own?" he asked. "She's looking for her sister. She might have gone through profiles from her sister's dating app. You said that was the reason you'd stopped by. It couldn't be that difficult for her to locate me, as well."

Lawler issued a sharp sigh. He wasn't thrilled, but he couldn't stop her or arrest her for looking into her sister's disappearance.

"She could have hired her own investigator, which would have been a bigger pain for you," Morgan pointed out when the sheriff didn't respond. The wheels were turning. That much was obvious. "We're all on the same team here. If one of your siblings was in the same situation, would you sit back and wait or would you go looking for them?"

Lawler's jaw clenched.

"I know what I'd do," Morgan said. "And I believe you'd do the same."

∾

Avril was cleared of any injuries, so she rejoined Morgan and the sheriff. If she was going to get her backside chewed out, she needed to get it over with, so she could resume looking for Mazie. Avril's nerves were jacked up on adrenaline and there was no way she was going to be able to sleep now.

"Sheriff," she began, but he cut her off with a severe look.

"I might understand why you took it upon yourself to visit a potential suspect," he said with a warning look, "but make no mistake about it, I'll arrest you myself if you interfere with this investigation."

"I'm just trying to cooperate," she countered, placing a balled fist on her hip. It was probably the wrong move because the sheriff blew out a frustrated sigh and looked one step away from slapping cuffs on her.

Avril put her hands up in the surrender position, palms out. "I'm sorry, Sheriff. I probably shouldn't have stopped by Mr. Firebrand's house this evening, but I'm looking for my sister too. So far, law enforcement hasn't found answers or my sister. Correct me if I'm wrong, but we have two departments cooperating and essentially no leads."

"You might be putting yourself in danger, Ms. Capri," the sheriff said. "I don't want you to go missing as well."

"Do you have a sister?" Avril asked.

"No, ma'am," the sheriff said. "I have a brother."

"Then, I don't think you can understand," Avril stated. "My baby sister lost our mother when she was way too young and then ended up bounced around in foster care because no judge would give her to me, even though I would have done a better job. We might have struggled, but we would have figured it out. Together. She's been on a good path for a few years now. She was thinking about setting down roots instead of moving around every few months. And now she's missing. Gone. Just like that. And, once again, I wasn't there to protect her." She could feel anger and frustration rising like water toward its boiling point. "So, you tell me. If you'd let your family member down every step of the way, would you just sit back after she went missing?"

She glanced over at Morgan, who'd bowed his head. He stared at the ground like it held the answers to the world's biggest questions, and he had ten seconds to figure it all out.

"I'd let the law do its job," Lawler said without conviction. Even he had to realize how out of the realm of possibility that would be for any caring person.

"Would you?" Avril pressed because his body language shifted and he didn't make eye contact when he spoke.

He gave a small headshake, almost imperceptible.

"The last thing I need is to be searching for two missing persons," he finally said with a little more feeling. That statement, she believed.

"Understood," she said, capitalizing on his softer side. "It's the reason I texted myself before I went inside Mr. Firebrand's home." She flashed eyes at him when his gaze lifted to briefly meet hers. Even then, even now, when sex was the last thing on her mind, a trill of awareness shot through her the second their eyes met. The air between them crackled with electricity. Breaking eye contact did little to stop it or settle the goosebumps on her arms.

Reality brought her focus back to the sheriff.

"That was smart," Lawler said. "But I wish you'd reached out to me first."

"Would you have told me to go in the first place?" she asked, knowing full well he wouldn't. "Or would you have given me the same line you did a few minutes ago?"

Lawler didn't answer. Instead, he said, "It's my job to warn you about interfering with an investigation."

"Technically, you said we don't know if a crime has been committed yet," she reminded. "I'm cooperating at this point and grateful for everything you're doing."

"Where are you headed next?" the sheriff asked.

"I don't have a car," she said.

"I'll take you wherever you need to go," Morgan said before the sheriff could speak up.

Sheriff Lawler studied Morgan.

"I'm knee-deep in this investigation, whether I want to be or not," Morgan explained. "At least if she's with me, there will be an extra layer of protection around her. Plus, now that you know we'll be together, it would be all kinds of stupid on my part for her to disappear on my watch. I have an added incentive to make sure she stays in one piece."

Lawler opened his mouth to speak and then clamped it shut almost as quickly. He nodded. "I'm not agreeing to any of this. However, you have a right to follow up on your family member. I'd just like to put on record that we'll get a lot more done if we work together."

"Agree," Avril said, not looking a gift horse in the mouth.

"Where to next?" Morgan asked.

"My sister's apartment in Austin," she said. Could the three of them find answers there?

4

The tow truck pulled away as Morgan walked Avril to his vehicle. The sheriff had agreed to follow them to Austin, despite the late hour. As much as Morgan thought Avril needed sleep, he also realized it would be next to impossible for her right now while she was pumped full of adrenaline.

At some point, however, she would crash. He didn't mind being there to catch her when she fell. If he was smart, he would pull away now while he still had the chance. Maybe it was those blue orbs or the lost quality to them that sucked him in. The reason didn't matter, he was all in until they found her sister. For her sake, he prayed they would find Mazie alive. The all-too-familiar guilt in Avril's voice a minute ago had been a gut punch. On a deep level, he could relate.

After opening the door to the passenger side, he came round the front of the truck and then claimed the driver's seat.

"Thank you," Avril said.

"No problem," he said as he navigated onto the highway, heading south.

"I've been nothing but a problem for you since I showed up," she said quietly. "And I intend to figure out a way to repay the kindness you've shown."

"I'd be offended if you did," he countered. "Believe it or not, I'm not doing any of this for you. It's nothing I wouldn't do for any good person who showed up at my door needing a hand up."

"Cowboy code," she said in a tone that gave him the impression he'd just offended her.

He hadn't meant for that to happen. Nor did he plan to give away the unexpected surge of attraction he felt every time she was near. "Something like that."

Avril tapped her index finger on the armrest. "You asked if my sister had a history of disappearing."

"Yes," he confirmed, noticing the change in topic.

"She does," Avril said. "It's the reason I didn't call the police in Austin right away. I should have taken it more seriously from day one, but I didn't."

"You couldn't have known this time would be different," he said, with a little more heat than intended.

From the corner of his eye, he noticed the look she fired at him.

"Have you forgiven yourself yet?" she asked, once again catching him off guard.

"About?"

"What's going on with your mother," she said with a sympathetic glance.

"What makes you think I—"

"You understand me in a way no one else does," she said, cutting him off. "You wouldn't be able to do that without having been through the same kind of guilt."

Or maybe they were just kindred spirits, twin flames. He'd never believed in the concept until meeting her. Until now.

"Either way, I'm interested to see what we find at your sister's place," he said. It was his turn to guide the conversation. "I'm guessing you've been there already."

"I have," she said, going with the change in direction, "but I'm hoping fresh eyes will see something I missed."

"What about Austin PD?" he asked.

"The officer took a couple of steps inside, turned around twice, and then walked right back out the door," she informed. "He'd asked if my sister had ever disappeared before and I was honest with my answer. Too honest. And now look where we are."

"He thought she hooked up with a guy and took off?" he asked to confirm.

The finger-tapping rhythm hit double time. "Afraid so."

"It's a big department," he stated, even though she'd probably already figured that out.

"The officer said this happened frequently with the number of college students at UT," she said. "Parents call and request wellness checks when their kids are really just on benders or skipping school to hit the lake. They don't answer their cell or respond to texts for a couple of hours and the parent panics."

"Someone like Sheriff Lawler would take this situation a whole more serious," he pointed out.

"He's actually the only one I feel like might be taking this seriously so far," she said on an exacerbated sigh.

Austin PD's response also explained why she felt the need to put herself in harm's way to find her sister.

"No one is making any promises," she said. "Austin said they'd have a unit patrol around her apartment in case she showed up. They finally put out a call after I bugged them almost every day for a week."

He couldn't imagine the panic and fear that must have set in by then. "Does your sister have any hobbies? Fishing? Hunting?"

"More like thrift store shopping," she said, her voice a little lighter. "It's one of the things we used to do together, when I would get permission to pick her up from one of her foster homes."

Not exactly a place someone goes to in order to disappear. The other obvious point was that some bastard had made a fake profile of him for the express intention of abducting a female. Since his name was used, he couldn't help but fear Mazie might be caught up in a revenge plot against his family. Or could she be a willing participant? Could she be part of a scam? She had to know her sister would move heaven and earth to find her.

No, this had to be a real abduction. Nothing else made sense. Unless...

Could this be part of a publicity stunt on her part? A way to gain new followers?

"Have you checked her subscription base since the disappearance?" he asked, hoping that wasn't the case.

"No," she admitted. "Why?"

"But you did mention she was MIA to her subscribers."

"I mean, yes, but I'm not sure I see the point," she said. And then recognition dawned. "Oh. You think my sister might have assumed I would look for her? Put something on her site?" She grabbed her cell from her handbag and studied the screen. "Holy hell."

He waited for the number.

"She has gained close to fifty thousand subscribers." Avril sat there, still...dumbfounded? "My sister can be flighty, which was the reason I gave her time to turn up on her own. But this? I find it hard to imagine she would stoop so low."

"Local PD is probably watching these numbers," he said. "It could be another reason they aren't as enthusiastic about throwing resources at the investigation."

"All the more reason to keep digging ourselves," she said. "I have no proof and you certainly have no reason to trust my word. But the sister I knew wouldn't do something like this for attention."

"Could she be highlighting how dangerous it is to use dating apps?" he asked.

"Her channel is entertaining," she said. "She makes up little skits and wears silly clothes. She takes on a persona. I've never once seen her take up a hotbed topic or try to make a point. She said she likes the work because it lets her be another person."

Meaning she didn't have to be herself. The concept was deep but he had to agree with Avril. A disappearing act seemed out of character based on what he'd learned about Mazie so far. It might be good to dig into her channel a little deeper.

"What about her neighbors?" he asked. "Did she know them or interact with them often?"

"There were parties in the building," she said. "It's downtown Austin and she lives in a loft apartment with shared rooftop space."

Should he know what that meant?

His expression must have given away his confusion because she added, "Lots of single, young adults in one building. She's mentioned having to get on neighbors for noise when she's trying to film."

"The sheriff might want to talk to folks in her building," Morgan pointed out. "I'd like to hear from them as well."

"I knocked on doors and asked whoever answered when the last time they saw my sister was," she said. "Didn't get anything useful from anyone."

"The person we're looking for might not have ever been a visitor," he said. That would be harder to track down. But they had to start somewhere.

~

THE DRIVE FLEW by while Avril talked to Morgan. The sheriff followed, despite the late hour. She could only hope his investigative skills could uncover something she'd overlooked at the apartment.

Traffic in downtown Austin was bad. Always bad. Day or night, cars and people were everywhere in this town. It was one of the main reasons she'd chosen to live in a nearby suburb north of the city. The location near Round Rock gave her access to events but kept her out of the day-to-day traffic grind.

As much as having her car totaled sucked, and it did, she didn't want to be alone after what happened to her on the road. Her nerves were fried and she wouldn't be able to sleep even if she tried. Plus, this felt like forward motion when her investigation had been stagnant for days.

"Foster care must have been hard on Mazie," Morgan said out of the blue. "I was just thinking about how complicated families can be. And yet, going into the unknown with people she didn't know must have been scary."

"Mazie used to beg me to keep her on the days I was allowed visitation," Avril admitted. The memories still broke her heart despite all these years later. Tears pricked the backs of her eyes. She tucked her chin to her chest and sniffled, giving herself a second to regain her composure before continuing.

Morgan steered with his left hand, using his right to reach out to touch her hand. He gave a surprisingly gentle squeeze. His touch was a mix of reassurance and spark. As much as she didn't want to let it be, their chemistry was a force unto itself. Was she attracted to Morgan? Maybe a better question was, who wouldn't be? But this wasn't the time for an inconvenient attraction, no matter how much her body, mind, and soul argued otherwise.

Plus, she'd learned a long time ago not to put stock in relationships. She was happily single.

A voice in the back of her mind wanted to point out that she wasn't as happy as she was trying to convince herself she was. She could admit there were times when loneliness crept in. But depending on her dad had been a joke. Her mother didn't leave them on purpose, and yet she was gone all the same. Mazie tried to depend on Avril, and look where that had gotten her sister. Having a family of her own wasn't something Avril sat around and dreamed about. Ever. In fact, she thought having a family was an awful thing to do to people.

Of course, she heard the irony in her own statement. Families were great for some. Just not her. She couldn't bear to let anyone else down, and she would. If anyone doubted her, all they had to do was take a look at her track record.

"I'm sorry she went through the system and had bad experience after bad experience," he said. "It's not supposed to be like that."

She shrugged, not able to let those words penetrate for fear the dam might break and she might start crying. If she started, she might not stop.

"And it wasn't fair to you either," he continued like he was completely unaware of the fact those words could unravel her.

"It's the way it is," she said in as flat a voice as she could manage. "It could have happened to anyone."

"But it didn't," he said. "It happened to you and your sister."

Going down that road would only lead to more heartache and pain, so she was relieved when he pulled into the underground parking garage in Mazie's building.

"Your sister must have been doing well for herself to be able to afford a place here," he said.

"She was…is," she said, correcting herself. "I used to teach self-defense in a classroom, which didn't pay a whole lot but it was the kind of work I wanted to do after burning out as a nurse. One day, my sister talked me into posting videos online, which now brings in enough income for me to live comfortably. The best part is that I can reach more women, and men, this way. But, honestly, most of my views are from women, and advertisers pay for that audience."

"It's pretty smart," he said. "Sounds like it gives you a lot of freedom to move around and not be tied to a desk."

"It does," she said. "But I wouldn't have that without Mazie. She was the one who talked me into taking my business online."

"The most we have online is ranch business, which I have nothing to do with," he admitted. "I barely use my phone since I'm on land where there's no coverage most of the time, and I refuse to carry a satellite phone. No one needs to contact me so much that they can't wait until I'm done for the day."

"No wife?" she asked, but she'd already checked for a

wedding band. Her heart gave a little leap when none was there.

He shook his head.

Relief washed over her. She'd wanted to know the answer more than she probably should.

"You?"

"Sounds like a blessing and a curse that you aren't checking your phone every five seconds," she said, ignoring his question along with the trill of excitement that came with the knowledge he was single. "It's easy to get addicted to checking for 'likes' or subscribers."

"How does it work with viewers?" he asked, letting her get away with the non-answer. "Is it the same?"

"I'm not sure I follow," she said.

"I was just thinking a subscriber might have become obsessed with your sister," he said.

"There are definitely creeps out there," she admitted. "I filter through them easily, and, honestly, I don't have the kind of following she does. I get the occasional creep."

"Has she mentioned anyone in particular?" he asked.

"Not really," she said. "She's only ever talked in general terms. But we can check her laptop once we get upstairs. Her car is missing."

He navigated into a visitor's parking spot. The sheriff pulled in a few seconds later, taking the open spot next to them.

"Sounds like it might be a good place to start," he said with a reassuring nod.

"Now you have me thinking in a whole new direction," she said. Someone, a subscriber, with computer skills might be smart enough to use a VPN from the diner in Lone Star Pass or enter the numbers. The sheriff had explained how it was all possible, but Avril was lucky to post her videos on her own. She didn't have near the online empire her sister, which also meant her needs were less complicated.

Empire might be a strong word. But still. Mazie was successful. She played characters. The dating app had thrown Avril in one direction. Could the person responsible have been commenting online right underneath their noses?

5

The wheels were turning. Morgan had heard about cyberstalking. He'd heard about cybercrimes. Somehow, he never figured he would be a target. Was it because of his very public last name? That was most likely a big part of it.

Could Mazie's apartment provide answers? If not answers, could it provide leads?

He hoped so, because he had an uneasy feeling that he couldn't seem to shake about the young woman's disappearance.

"Thank you for coming, Sheriff," Avril said, a newfound appreciation for the lawman in her voice.

Lawler tipped his hat. "Let's see what we can find inside."

It was the middle of the night. Ranchers would be up in another hour but most folks would be dead asleep right now. He meant to ask Avril where she'd been asking around about her sister in Lone Star Pass, to see if there was some kind of connection to be made there with her being followed. He would never have believed serious criminals could live in his hometown until the past few months, when a crime wave had been in full swing. Nowhere was immune these days. If school shooters could reach a small town like Uvalde, no one could let their guard down. The shootings had happened in an elementary school, no less. Anger shot through him at the senseless loss of life, and his heart broke for the families involved.

"Let's do this," the sheriff said, breaking into Morgan's heavy thoughts.

They followed Avril to the elevator bank. She tapped a keycard on a pad to get the elevator moving. The next thing he knew, they were on the fourth of four floors.

"My sister is 4D," she said, walking them to the door. Another key opened it, and then they were inside. There was a stillness in the place that was unsettling, as though the owner had gone on a long vacation. The air was stale, the lights off.

Avril tapped something on the wall to make them turn on in the kitchen, where the three of them stood. She walked through the space, tapping spots on the walls. The place didn't have traditional light switches. Give him a lamp any day. He knew how to work those. Living out on a ranch, it was impossible not to think he was missing out on much of the tech revolution. He tinkered around and could keep his laptop running fine. He knew when to replace his cell phone and how to install basic software on his computer. He was techie enough to know not to install virus protection software, but rather use his firewall instead.

That was about the extent of his computer skills. He also knew that he could figure out how to do almost anything, as long as he had access to the internet.

So, living in a new smart home held no appeal. He'd never considered it hard to flip a switch if he needed light in a room. Didn't figure that would change. Although voice activation was a cool new trick he would consider.

Once the lights were on, he walked around, surveying the environment. The kitchen showed signs of someone living here. There was a half-eaten loaf of bread on the counter. It was moldy. There were crumbs around the opening of the bread bag.

The open concept space left very little to the imagination. The room was large with high ceilings, no doubt a perk that came with living on the top floor. There was a granite, no, marble island that had bar stools tucked around on three sides.

Mazie must be doing well to afford a place like this one in downtown Austin. Granted, this wasn't exactly New York City real estate, but this area of Austin was pricey. Plus, all the prices were rising in popular cities in Texas due to the influx of people flooding the state every few months. Lone Star Pass had been relatively untouched as a population, which also meant there were no new people in town to date. Given the twenty-four-seven nature of the cattle ranching business, it had been easy to slip into a routine that didn't include dating.

Sheriff Lawler walked around, taking notes and poking various items that had been abandoned on the counter with the end of a pencil. He glanced over. "Don't touch anything."

"Got it," Morgan said by way of reassurance. He hadn't intended to, in case this place turned into a crime scene, which would happen if a body showed up.

The sheriff took out a paper bag and tucked a few items inside that Morgan didn't get a look at. He figured the hunt for fingerprints other than Mazie's was on.

Nothing looked so out of place that someone left

forcibly. There were no signs of struggle. Just an untidy apartment, except for one corner of the room.

The serious tripod, holding a professional quality camera, pointed toward the corner where Mazie must film. There was a desk pushed against the opposite wall that had a couple of used Coke cans sitting on top, as well as a stack of unopened mail.

He walked over and checked it out. Not being able to touch the envelopes made it impossible to know what might be inside.

The professional setup was missing one important thing...a computer.

"Did you say your sister used a laptop?" he asked Avril, who was looking around in the designated bedroom area where clothes were in piles on the floor and the bed was unmade. The whole apartment was one big contrast with the pristine work area taking up a good chunk of the living room space. Anything out of camera view was messy. The place wasn't filthy, other than the old cans. It didn't smell like day-old pizza. It was in disarray. Would she have invited someone here on a date?

Most folks put their best foot forward, so he doubted she would bring someone into the space when it looked like this. Was this place a dead end?

"Looks the same as when I was here last week," Avril said. "And, yes, to answer your question, she worked off a laptop that's always plugged in right..."

She froze.

"I didn't notice that before," she said. "Her laptop was always plugged in. She said her phone was for everything else."

"The fact it's missing now doesn't prove an abduction," Lawler said as he walked over.

Behavior rarely changed unless there was a reason.

"As soon as the sun's up, we can ask neighbors if they saw anyone coming and going out of this apartment, with or without Mazie," the sheriff continued.

Avril nodded. "I asked before if anyone saw my sister with someone new, but maybe we can dig deeper to question roommates."

"At this point, I'd be willing to grill random people in the elevator," Morgan said.

"There are no security cameras in the building," Lawler pointed out. "I called the management company to ask."

"None in the parking garage either?" Morgan asked, thinking that was strange. Then again, he had a preconceived idea that every building in a bigger city had cameras everywhere.

Lawler shook his head. "Said they would have had to raise the rents even higher to have the cameras monitored, not to mention the cost of equipment, so the residents took a hard pass."

"That's surprising," Avril said.

"Visitor parking isn't monitored but you saw the barrier to get into resident parking," Lawler said.

"And the fact I had to use a card key to get the elevator going," Avril added.

"It might be best if I make the rounds with the neighbors while I'm here," Lawler said. "It's the middle of the week in the middle of the night. I've had good luck with folks answering under similar circumstances."

Avril crossed her arms over her chest, a defensive move. She bit down on her bottom lip as her forehead wrinkled in concern. "Any chance we can go with you?"

"It's best if I go alone since this is official business," Lawler said. "I'll send a report back."

Avril's nod came after a few seconds of silence.

The sheriff excused himself, and then left.

"Is it wrong that I want to follow him anyway, to spy?" she asked.

"Not wrong, but it might be criminal," Morgan pointed out. Sticking around here much longer wouldn't do any good. He glanced around one more time, figuring Avril was about to ask for a ride home.

"This might sound like a random question, but can I stay with you tonight?"

∼

"Yes," Morgan answered.

Avril didn't realize she was holding her breath, waiting for him to answer, until she exhaled. "Thank you. I can't imagine being alone after what happened on the highway a little while ago."

"You don't have a car now either," he said. "You'd be stuck waiting around for a car service if you use one of those apps. Plus, it could get expensive."

"To add insult to injury, I'd never be able to relax enough here to sleep," she said, as relief washed over her. He might have said earlier that he would see this through because his name had been brought into the picture, but she was grateful for his help anyway. He might not be pitching in for her, but she benefited. It had been too long since anyone had her back. So much so, she could barely believe it was true, despite mounting evidence he had no plans to walk away.

Morgan was the real deal. He was honest and genuine. The way her heart hammered the inside of her ribcage when he was near and her pulse climbed had her wishing they'd met under different circumstances. Then again, she would never go out with a man like him, no matter how much her heart tried to convince her that he'd be different. That fact was half the problem because she could see herself falling for him, and her heart shattering into a million tiny flecks of dust when it was over. And it *would* end.

All relationships had a shelf life. Avril could only let herself go so far before she had to put on the brakes. Self-preservation required it and she had no plans to fall into the trap of believing in fairy tale relationships. Just ask her sister.

Avril's heart ached at how long Mazie had been missing. The likelihood her sister would turn up shrank every hour of her continued disappearance. Avril couldn't risk letting the tiny balloon of hope shrivel up. The guilt would be unbearable.

"Ready?" Morgan's calm, masculine voice broke through her heavy thoughts.

She didn't realize she'd zoned out as she stared at the camera setup. "Yes. Let's go."

The sheriff must've moved onto the next floor, because there was no sign of him anywhere on the fourth after Avril locked up.

Side by side, she walked with Morgan to the elevator. As the doors opened, his hand came up to the small of her back. His touch was gentle and clearly not meant as sexual, and yet her skin reacted like they were on a date, and he'd touched her for the first time. Her breath caught and her stomach free fell with contact.

This man was exactly the kind of dangerous that had been missing in every guy she'd dated in her teens, twenties, and now early thirties. It was the kind that made her want to see how it played out, rather than run, because she'd never experienced sensations like these before.

Morgan was helping her. He was taking pity on her. He was keeping an eye on the investigation. The man wasn't trying to seduce her.

Keeping her feelings in check had never been a problem for Avril in the past. She'd been nicknamed 'Ice Queen' by more than one of her past boyfriends. The first who'd said it, Mitch, had teased her that he was just playing and didn't mean it when she'd taken offense. She'd let the nickname slide until she'd overheard him telling one of his friends that he was at the Ice Queen's house.

After Mitch, there'd been Blake. It might have been a new man and two years since her last relationship, but the nickname came back to haunt her. *Ice Queen.* She'd overheard him talking to his brother when he'd first used the term. When Peter, boyfriend number three, came up with the same nickname, she'd decided no more boyfriends. Casual dating kept things light, and no one got close enough to offend her again. Since turning thirty-three, she'd been happily single. Well, single if not happy.

Plus, so what if she was an ice queen? Wasn't that better than falling apart every five seconds? Or falling in love with every guy she met? And one more thing, maybe she hadn't met a man strong enough to handle her or hot enough to melt the ice.

Until Morgan, a little voice in the back of her mind felt the need to point out.

Inside the truck, she stretched the seatbelt over her and then clicked it securely into place.

"Tell me what kind of person your sister normally dated," Morgan said as he started the engine and then navigated out of the visitor section of the garage onto the street.

"She didn't introduce me to her boyfriends," Avril said. "I know that probably sounds odd, but she was busy and hadn't dated in a long time." Or so she'd said. Could there have been someone else in the background?

"How close were the two of you, if you don't mind my asking," he said.

"We checked in at least once a week and tried to get together in person on a monthly basis," she said. When she heard it like that, it didn't sound like much. Had she been an ice queen with her sister as well? Had she gotten so comfortable keeping people at a safe distance that she didn't realize she was doing the same to her own flesh and blood? "We talked about what was going on in each other's lives." She paused to really think about it because that didn't sound right. "Actually, I listened to what was going on in Mazie's life more so than shared what was going on in mine. She gave me the tip about putting my self-defense tips online, but I searched the rest on the internet to see how to start a business."

"We touched on Mazie possibly having a rabid fan or two earlier," he said with a nod. "This might be a good time to pick up the possibility again. Take it seriously once we get back to the cabin."

She stretched out her legs and straightened her back as her eyes blurred.

"You have a laptop," she said. "We can start there once we..." Actually, why wait? She located her cell and then scrolled. "I don't know what I was thinking." She bit back a yawn. "I have my phone right here and it'll be fine for scrolling. What am I looking for exactly?"

"Top commenters," he said. "Particularly males."

"My sister has a big following, with a lot of engagement," she said. "This is like searching for a needle in a haystack. If

I had her login information, I could approach this from another angle. Most websites have analytics that can detail out the information."

"Is that something the sheriff can dig into?" he asked.

"I'm not exactly sure how any of that works on the legal end," she said. "But it's a good question to ask." She fired off a text to the lawman. "I should also probably know the answer for my own business's sake." Funny how starting a business was such a monumental task she'd never even thought about a possibility like this. Most small businesses existed on a wing and a prayer, held together by good intentions and hard work. The learning curve was steep and the days long.

Avril glanced around at the vehicles on the road. One came close to clipping them, causing her pulse to race.

"Jerk," Morgan muttered as he swerved just in time. "City traffic is never my favorite, and Austin takes the cake."

"My sister walks a lot," Avril recalled. "Said she feels safer downtown because of all the activity. Between road traffic and UT, there's someone walking around at all hours of the night."

"She sounds like an interesting person," he said.

"Once you get to know her, she is," Avril said with a small smile. "Reckless too. But not in a self-destructive way. Mazie lives inside her own head. You know?"

He nodded but she wasn't sure he was following.

"I respect the way she doesn't care if someone doesn't like the clothes she's wearing or the way she styles her hair," Avril stated. "Even though she *is* sensitive. It's like she flips a switch when someone says or does something to hurt her. It rolls right off." Was that a trauma response?

Avril was beginning to look at her sister's actions in a

new light. Was Mazie in control or hiding? Was her sister as savvy as Avril believed or more naïve than she'd imagined?

Glancing in the sideview mirror sent a wave of panic rushing through her. "There's a big truck back there."

Was it *the* truck?

6

Morgan gripped the steering wheel a little tighter as he checked the rearview. "Can you be ready to call Lawler on a moment's notice?"

Avril sucked in a breath. "Yes."

"There's more than one oversized truck in Texas, especially in these parts now that we're on the highway," he said, hoping to calm her nerves while they were checking out the vehicle.

The driver came into the light.

"Looks like a group of college kids inside there," he said to her.

Avril exhaled a breath that was loaded with frustration. "Sorry."

"No reason to be," he said, loosening his grip back to normal on the wheel. "It's good to be on guard." He didn't add, *after what happened.* "You're on the right track, Avril. Probably getting close. Otherwise, you'd be left alone."

"That's the main reason I didn't want to go home tonight, even though my place is closer," she said. "I'm half afraid of what I'll find or who will be waiting for me."

"We'll hopefully hear from the sheriff soon," he said. "Maybe he'll have a direction. Until then, you're welcome to stay at my place as long as you like. I have a guest room that's empty."

"What about your girlfriend?" she asked. "I didn't see any pictures in your place earlier, but that doesn't mean you don't have someone expecting you."

"No girlfriend," he stated with a small headshake. "No need for one of those in my life." Now or ever. If he couldn't trust his own mother, who could he trust?

Morgan could be honest with himself enough to say no one had held his interest in longer than he cared to remember. He'd been burned enough times not to want to touch that fire again anyway.

"Why don't you lay your seat back and close your eyes?" he urged, figuring she might get some rest on the way back. She had to be beyond tired at this point.

The sun wasn't up yet but it would be by the time they arrived home. To *his* home, he corrected.

"Are you sure you don't want me to keep watch?" she asked, suppressing another yawn.

A quick glance over said her eyes were glued to the side-view mirror.

"I've got this for now," he said. "I'm used to no sleep and I've tracked enough poachers in my day to know how to watch my back."

"If you're sure," she said, but it was obvious she was barely hanging on. Adrenaline would have worn off by now, making staying awake while driving in the night even more difficult.

"I'm one hundred percent," he confirmed. It was clear that Avril would move heaven and earth to find her sister. The guilt she carried, over feeling like she'd let her sister down time and time again, was a weight on her shoulders. A burden he wished like anything he could ease.

Avril was intelligent, caring, and loyal. On top of those qualities, she was one of the most beautiful women he'd ever met, inside and out. She was determined, intense, and self-sufficient. Half of those qualities would be attractive. She was the total package.

She was also serious and guarded. The few times he'd gotten past her walls, he'd been shut out almost as quickly. To make matters worse, the instant he first saw her, it was like a lightning bolt struck him in the center of his chest. He'd been instantly attracted to her in a way like nothing he'd ever experienced.

But physical attraction wasn't enough to hold his interest for long. After talking to Avril, the pull toward her had intensified.

The last thing he could handle right now was a new relationship, what with the upheaval in his family and the pending trial for his mother. This was the worst possible timing. Not to mention the fact she wasn't there for social reasons. So, he was putting the proverbial cart before the horse going down this line of thinking anyway.

Avril's sister was missing. She'd been run off the road. Finding Mazie and the person responsible deserved their full attention. Even a slight distraction could get them both injured or worse.

Now that Avril was getting closer to an answer, which was the only explanation for someone targeting her, the bastard was coming for her. Morgan would be ready. No catching them off guard the next time around.

His thoughts bounced around for the rest of the ride to the cabin. By the time he pulled into the garage, the sun was shining. As the door closed behind him and he cut off the engine, Avril sat up ramrod straight with a gasp.

"You're okay," he soothed.

She glanced around almost frantically before her gaze landed on him and she almost instantly calmed down.

"Where are we?" she asked.

"Home," he said without thinking. Then, he quickly clarified, "My home." It was a little too easy to let the word *home* roll off his tongue when Avril was beside him.

The sound of a vehicle heading their way caused both to freeze. Their gazes locked. For a split second, time stopped.

Then, Morgan cleared his throat and jumped into action. He grabbed the Colt .45 that he kept hidden in his garage, a gun that he carried out on property in case he came across a coyote, and then exited through the garage's side door.

Coming down the drive was none other than his brother Nick, who looked all kinds of concerned.

Avril stood at the door directly behind Morgan, not committing to the garage or coming outside.

"Hold on a minute," she said from behind him as Nick parked. "I knew you had brothers, but you didn't tell me that you're a twin."

To be fair, they hadn't done a whole lot of talking about his side of the family other than a brief overview.

"Guess I'm too used to it to think of it as a novelty," Morgan said before lowering his gun and then tucking the weapon inside the waistband of his jeans in back.

Nick exited his Jeep, and then came around to his brother. "What? You don't answer calls anymore?" Nick's gaze bounced from Morgan to Avril. To his credit, he didn't ask any questions despite the flood of them in his eyes.

"I didn't get a call from you," Morgan said, reaching for

his cell. He fished the phone out of his breast pocket and checked the screen. "My bad." There were three missed calls from his brother. At some point overnight, he must have switched the sound off. When did that happen? He locked gazes with his brother because this couldn't be good. "What is it? What's going on?"

"You," Nick said. "I'm worried about you."

"I'm good," Morgan stated on an exhale.

"Which is why you haven't returned any of my texts over the past few days," Nick said in an accusing tone.

Morgan held up his phone. "Now those I didn't get. See for yourself."

"I'm Avril, by the way," Avril said, stepping out of the doorframe with an extended hand toward Nick.

Nick took the hand being offered and shook. "Nick Firebrand. Nice to make your acquaintance."

"What are you doing here?" Morgan asked a little more defensively than intended, cutting off the introductions.

"Checking up on you," Nick stated like the answer should be obvious. His brother sounded a little offended at the question.

Morgan held his hands up in the air. "See. I'm fine. No reason to be worried."

"Excuse me for caring," Nick retorted.

Damn. Morgan hadn't intended to be such a jerk.

"Hey, sorry," Morgan started. "Why don't you come inside and have a cup of coffee."

"I have chores to do," Nick responded. Twins had the kind of bond that made each other's emotions easy to read. Nick wasn't happy with Morgan, and he didn't have to be his twin to see it written on Nick's face.

"Can they wait a few minutes?" Morgan asked. "I'd like to run something past you."

Avril studied Nick.

"I guess so," Nick conceded.

"Good," Morgan said, bringing his brother into a bear hug. It was good to see him, even though Morgan didn't want to explain who Avril was or why she was staying at the cabin.

Letting his brother in on what was going on was probably a good idea. It never hurt to have extra eyes looking around, and the rest of the family needed to know if Morgan was bringing danger to them. Granted, his cabin was out in the middle of nowhere on the property but that didn't mean one of the family members wouldn't accidently step into harm's way.

All in all, he was glad his brother had agreed to come inside. And part of him liked Avril meeting the family.

~

Avril would have sworn she was seeing double, except Morgan's personality was different than Nick's. There was a steadiness to Morgan that came with quiet confidence. His smile, although rarely seen so far, had an indescribable radiance. Despite their same features, Morgan's hair was just a little longer and it made him more attractive. Still, there was a whole lot she didn't know about the Firebrand family, and Morgan. It was probably strange that she was put off by the fact he'd withheld the whole being a twin information from her, except that he'd become her lifeline in the past twelve hours. Not knowing he had a twin felt like a betrayal. And yet, the notion was unrealistic. He'd been thrown into this situation just as much as she had. He was going all-in to help. There wasn't a real reason she should be upset the subject of his sibling hadn't come up.

Still, it was a reminder to keep her guard up around Morgan. Because it was a little too easy to relax her defenses with him.

Coffee took next to nothing time to brew inside the kitchen. Everyone took a seat at the granite island after cups were filled.

"Are you sure you don't need to sleep?" Morgan asked her.

Avril found herself being genuinely touched by his concern. A growing part of her wanted to reach out to him, but she stopped herself. What good would it do? She didn't know the first thing about the man, if nothing else, the arrival of Nick had proven that.

"I'm good," she said. "The quick nap on the ride here helped a lot."

"When did you get here?" Nick asked, clearly confused about her presence. She shouldn't be offended. And yet, she was all the same.

"Yesterday," she admitted, not going into detail about the how and why she'd shown up. Morgan could go there if he wanted, but she didn't.

"How do the two of you know each other?" Nick asked. His surprise was written all over his face.

Avril wasn't sure if she should be flattered by Morgan's brother's reaction to her being at the cabin. It most likely meant he didn't bring people here very often. A tiny part of her felt satisfaction she couldn't afford to relish in.

"We're recent acquaintances," Morgan said. There was a protective quality to his tone that made her stomach free fall.

"Okay..." Nick said, drawing out the word.

Morgan leaned toward his brother. "Someone used my

name, picture, and details about my life to set up a fake dating account. Avril's sister responded and is missing."

"Wouldn't the law be able to figure out you didn't set up the profile?" Nick asked. He didn't question whether or not his brother might have set up the account. She took it as a sign of the trust between the two of them. In all the years she'd watched over Mazie, the two didn't have near the bond evident with Nick and Morgan. Then again, she'd always heard about the special twin bond. This was proof enough for her that it existed. Morgan gave a look that Nick seemed to understand without a whole lot of explaining.

Would she know what was on her sister's mind if they'd grown up together? The age gap combined with their mother's death had forced them into different homes and different paths. They'd found a deeper connection through running similar businesses after Mazie gave Avril the advice that changed her life. The timing of the pandemic brought viewers while everyone stayed indoors, looking for entertainment or a way to stay healthy during lockdown. The coincidence had caused many online businesses like theirs to boom.

"Whoever set up the profile made the location ping from the diner in town," Morgan said.

"I know enough about computers to realize the person could have played around with that," Nick said. "Doesn't mean they were actually in town."

"Right," Morgan agreed.

"How does that work?" Avril asked.

"The bastard could have tinkered with the numbers on the VPN," Morgan said. "I couldn't tell you how to do it, but I know it can be done."

Nick nodded.

"You should know someone ran Avril off the road after

she stopped by the cabin to ask a few questions," Morgan said to his brother. She appreciated the fact he didn't mention finding her rooting through his trash or how desperate she must have looked when he first encountered her.

Nick muttered a few choice words. The twins might look alike but spending a few minutes with them was all it took to be able to tell them apart. Morgan was t-shirt and jeans material whereas his brother wore long-sleeved flannel and cords. Their mannerisms were different too. Morgan had a habit of rubbing the scruff on his chin when he was thinking too hard. Nick, on the other hand, looked down at his boots and stared. He lifted his gaze to meet his brother's. "Do you want me to stick around while the two of you get some rest?"

"I couldn't sleep now if I tried," Avril admitted. "Plus, I dozed off on the way home. But Morgan hasn't slept."

"I'm good," Morgan said, waving them off.

"Are you sure? Because it's not normal to go without sleep for too long," she said, worried about him.

A small smile crossed both brothers' lips at the exact same moment. Twin bond?

She shot Morgan a curious look.

"During calving season, we don't sleep for days on end," he explained. "We get used to running on E in the sleep bank."

"Which is why my brother looks so much older than me," Nick said with a straight face. Then, broke into a wide smile.

Morgan laughed. Avril laughed. She couldn't remember the last time that happened. The last time she *really* laughed.

The comment broke some of the tension, which was also

a welcome change. Focusing on something so negative for this long couldn't be good. Plus, it never solved a problem. Shifting her attention was the best way to let an answer come to her instead of chasing one. Why did she always seem to forget this fact in stressful situations?

"Will you alert the family to what's going on?" Morgan asked his brother.

"I can do that," Nick said. "If I leave now, I'll be able to make the meeting."

Avril must've looked confused because Morgan spoke up.

"We have a meeting in the barn every morning with the ranch foreman," he explained. "We go over who is doing what for the day, so we don't end up covering the same ground."

"I'm impressed that you guys work together so well," she said.

Both men laughed.

"Being cooperative is new to this group," Morgan explained. "Our mother is in jail right now for trying to cut the other side of the family out of our grandfather's will. She went too far."

"Have you been to see her?" Nick asked as the air in the room suddenly changed at the mention of their mother.

"No," Morgan admitted. "You?"

"I keep meaning to but never seem to get there," Nick said as he stood up. He drained his coffee cup before walking over and placing it inside the sink.

"I know what you mean," Morgan agreed, the all-too familiar ring of guilt in his tone.

Avril should know.

"It's none of my business, and I certainly don't know anything about your situation other than what's on the internet," she started. "But you might never forgive yourself if you don't make an attempt to stop by."

"She's guilty," Morgan said, stiffening.

"And yet, that doesn't change the fact she's still your mother," Avril said. Pushing the boundaries of one of the few people in her corner didn't seem like her best idea.

"We can't deny that much," Morgan said before issuing a long pause. "The real question is, what would we say to her?"

7

The subject of Jackie Firebrand had been off limits. Morgan wasn't the stand-on-the-fence type, but he'd never been more conflicted in his life. His relationship with his mother fell into the category of *complicated*.

Morgan didn't do complicated. He preferred an easy life with few entanglements. Hell, even his cabin was neat.

"All I can say is that I would trade almost anything for one more day with my mother," Avril stated with a shrug. "But I know it doesn't always work that way for everyone, and I have no judgment about your situation."

"The two of you must have been close," Nick said. She seemed suddenly aware of just how tuned in to the conversation Morgan's brother was.

"I blamed her for my father ditching the family," she said. "And then I got really angry when Mom got sick. Until then, I'd mostly ignored her requests to get together." She stared out the window for a long moment. "I don't know how I would feel about her, about *me*, if I hadn't had the chance to talk to her and apologize. If that hadn't happened and she'd died, I would have regretted it for the rest of my life."

"Not everyone gets closure," Morgan pointed out. "I'm glad it worked out for you, though."

"No," she said on a soft sigh. "Not everyone gets the 'I'm sorry and I love you', or the 'I messed up and I love you', but you'll never know if you don't try. And if you try but it doesn't work out, you'll still have the peace of knowing you did everything you could. At least you'll be able to walk away with a clear conscience. And I'm sorry this is happening in your family. I can't imagine what you must be going through."

Morgan didn't immediately speak. Both him and his twin stood there, contemplating those words. Had they struck the same chord with Nick as they did with Morgan?

"I better get on my way if I'm going to make the meeting," Nick finally said, but there was a deeper quality to his voice. Morgan had heard it before when Nick was stuffing down his emotions.

Morgan was doing the same, so he couldn't exactly condemn his brother. Families were complicated. The Firebrands didn't do anything small. So the big feelings stirred up inside him shouldn't surprise him as much as they did.

"I'll see you later," Morgan said to his brother.

Nick nodded. He took a couple of steps before doubling back and bringing Morgan into a bear hug. "Take care, okay?"

"You know I will," Morgan said, embracing his brother.

Nick cleared his throat before taking a step back and extending a hand toward Avril. "It was nice getting to know you."

"Same," she said, taking the offering. Nick pulled her into a brief hug.

"Take care of him," his brother whispered.

Morgan didn't point out that he'd heard Nick before he left. Their relationship had been strained but was getting on good footing again. Hell, almost everyone's relationships had been under duress since their grandfather's death. Even before that, if Morgan was being honest about the situation. Especially before that if he was being totally honest. They'd come together recently, but his mother was still behind bars for a crime he couldn't begin to fathom. Avril was right about what she'd said, though. He might be haunted for the rest of his life if he didn't at least clear the air with Jackie Firebrand.

Where did he start?

Right now though, he had something else that required his full attention. Losing Avril wasn't an option, so he needed to shove his emotions aside when it came to the mess his mother was in. When Mazie was safely back home and Avril was out of danger, which was the only outcome he could let himself believe until proven otherwise, he would swing by the jail to set the record straight. Kicking someone when they were down wasn't his style, so he would have to finesse his way through the conversation. Talking wasn't exactly his forte, but it came easily with Avril. She was beginning to open up to him, and he surprised himself in wanting to know more about her.

The case might depend on a piece of information she could supply. So far, the investigation had begun by focusing on him. Once he'd cleared up the facts, the law had shifted to searching for answers back in Austin with her neighbors. And then it dawned on him that Avril had mentioned an obsessed fan along with a computer guy. "Did you say you have contact information for Mazie's tech guy?"

Morgan grabbed his laptop and powered it up.

He looked over at Avril, who was nursing a cup of coffee. Shoulders forward, she didn't look up.

"She always referred to him as her tech guy," she said. "I never asked his name since we didn't live close to each other, but I got the impression he stayed busy."

"Maybe the sheriff can dig around her cell records and find him," Morgan said. He would like to be the one to speak to the man, but at least the sheriff would. He was a skilled investigator, so he would most likely be able to get the information they were looking for. Morgan didn't care how the bastard responsible was found, just that Mazie was located before it was too late.

"Is it wrong that I want to put a notice up on my sister's channel?" she asked.

"Can you do that?" he asked. "Do you have access to her channel?"

"Not to put up a video, but I can always say something in the chat section," she said. Then, she cursed. "Except she might moderate comments. In which case, my comment would sit in the queue."

"Would someone as successful as your sister hire someone to manage those details?" he asked.

"I doubt it," she said. "Unless her tech guy does it."

"Check to see when the last comment was made on her most recent upload," he said, pushing the laptop toward her.

She took the offering and pulled up her sister's site.

Avril smacked the granite with the flat of her palm. "Bingo. Comments are coming through, past her disappearance date."

"That's good news," he said. It was the first break they'd had so far and her smile was worth every minute of the effort. A sense of satisfaction struck like another bolt of lightning that he'd been the one to put the smile there.

"What do I say?" she asked but he could tell she was thinking out loud. Her lips compressed and her index finger came up to her chin. Her eyes unfocused like she was looking inside herself for the right answer.

Morgan usually got straight to the point when it came to communication. He wasn't exactly known for his finesse. He figured Avril was asking a rhetorical question anyway, so he refrained from making a comment.

The glimmer of hope in her eyes concerned him. It was too early. A real human might not be approving the posts. There could be a filter system setup through an app. Morgan had no idea how such a thing would work on a coding level but it seemed like there was an app for just about everything. Filtering through comments using keywords to make sure no vitriol comments got through didn't seem like it would require coding genius. It was still above his pay grade where computers were concerned, but his knowledge ended with how to operate one on a basic level.

Avril refocused on the screen and sat up a little straighter. "I know what to say."

∼

W*here is* Trix $

Those three words along with a dollar sign weren't rocket science but they should hopefully get Avril's point across.

She hit enter and sat back, waiting to see if her comment would post right away. She took in a deep breath and held it.

"What happened?" Morgan asked, scooting a chair beside her as she released the breath she'd been holding.

This close, she breathed in his warm, masculine scent. It

reminded her of something...sandalwood? There was something about his earthy scent that caused her body to warm as she breathed.

Three dots on the screen shocked her attention back to the computer. And then her comment popped up.

"That was fast," she said, disheartened.

Morgan studied the screen. "Trix?"

"My sister doesn't use her real name for her channel," she said.

"Why didn't I notice that earlier?" he asked. "Interesting."

"What do you think? Is there someone behind the curtain?" she asked.

"I doubt it," he said. "If she had a person back there, I doubt they would be up this early, watching for comments to come through to approve."

Avril issued a sharp sigh. "You're right. I guess I got my hopes up over nothing."

"We'll catch a break," he said. "We just have to be patient a little while longer."

She nodded, but there was no enthusiasm in her movement.

"Have you heard from the sheriff on the neighbors?" he asked, clearly searching for better news.

She shook her head. "He promised to keep us posted before he left though."

"He might not have anything to report," Morgan pointed out.

"I was afraid of that," she said. "Even though I asked around the building already, I was hoping he would have better luck. I figured a badge could get people talking, remembering."

"The bastard we're looking for might not have ever been invited to her apartment," Morgan said.

That actually made sense. "True. I seriously doubt Mazie would bring a stranger home. She didn't take her safety lightly."

"All the more reason to look in her inner circle for the answers," he said.

Avril needed to get the name of the guy who took care of Mazie's computer. Maybe he knew something. "Except that she said she'd met someone recently. I distinctly remember her saying those exact words."

"Which brings us back to the online dating," Morgan said. "And the fake profile."

"It's frustrating," she said. "I feel stuck in a never-ending loop."

Out of the corner of her eye, she saw responses rolling in. Twenty-six comments turned into thirty-seven in what felt like the blink of an eye. And the numbers kept increasing.

"Looks like you stirred up the pot," Morgan said.

She skimmed the responses. "Most folk seem genuinely concerned about my sister's whereabouts. Some of these are cold-hearted."

Her cell buzzed. She reached for it and then checked the screen. "Hello, Sheriff."

"I thought we had an agreement that you would sit tight, and allow me the room to do my job," he said with clear frustration in his tone.

"We're on the same team here," she said, putting the call on speaker so Morgan could hear. "And I never made a promise to sit back and do nothing. I'm sorry if you got that impression based on our past conversations."

"I have someone watching the site for unusual activity," he continued, like he didn't hear her protest.

"Maybe this will give them something to work with," she said by way of defense.

"Or confuse the issue," he said. "We were looking for someone who was watching the site while it was inactive."

"Oh," she said. This mistake might have cost valuable time in locating her sister. More of that familiar guilt slammed into her.

"Promise me you'll leave well enough alone," he said.

Avril bit down on her bottom lip. "You have my word."

"In the spirit of cooperation, I canvassed the neighbors but no one saw anything suspicious," he said. "Of course, the trail is cold by now. Most folks have a hard time remembering what they ate for breakfast, so it was too much to hope they could recall information that was a couple of weeks old."

A cold trail wasn't good. Avril knew that.

"What do we do next?" she asked.

"I'll keep at it," he said. "I have a detective in Austin who is finally eager to cooperate."

Sure, now that the sheriff was involved, Austin PD was taking this case seriously. Where was that enthusiasm when Avril had begged them to get involved?

To be fair, they had put the information out about Mazie and started looking into her disappearance. Without them, the sheriff wouldn't be involved and they wouldn't be making any progress. Though progress felt like an ambitious word to describe their slow crawl towards information.

"That sounds promising," she said. Avril didn't normally stretch the truth but she wanted it to be true so she'd gone with the first thing that came to mind.

"I don't want to get your hopes up," Lawler said. "Rest

assured we'll do everything in our power to get the answers you deserve."

Avril was far less encouraged after that last statement. It was the sheriff essentially telling her to prepare to identify her sister's body when this thing was over, rather than prepare to welcome her home.

A glance over at Morgan revealed he was likely thinking the same thing.

"Thank you," Avril said because nothing else came to mind. At least the sheriff was digging around. Dig long enough and he'd find something. He had to. "But you should know that I plan to continue to search for my sister."

"I was afraid you'd say something like that," he said. "Watch your back, don't cross any lines, and we'll get along fine. I'd hate to have to lock you up to keep you out of danger."

"That would be a violation of my rights and we both know it," she said. "I'm allowed to look for her, Sheriff. And I couldn't live with myself if I didn't do everything in my power to find her."

A heavy sigh came across the line.

"Keep me informed," he directed before ending the call before she could tell him goodbye.

Tension corded her muscles until it felt like they might snap. She set the phone on the granite before flexing and releasing her fingers a few times to free some of the stress in her body.

Morgan swiveled her chair around until she faced him. His powerful thighs bracketed her legs. "We'll find her. I promise."

Was it a promise he could keep?

Avril had no idea, but she held onto those words like

they were a raft in the middle of a stormy sea. "I can't afford to give up hope."

"There's no reason to," he said with the kind of reassurance that almost had her believing everything would work out, despite evidence to the contrary.

Avril lifted her gaze to meet his, and then held. Her stomach free fell, as though she'd gone cliff diving, as she looked into those sincere eyes. Thick lashes framed the brightest shade of blue. His was a face of hard planes, but his eyes had a compassionate quality that stirred feelings deep in her chest. Those feelings couldn't afford to surface.

"Feel free to say no," she said, almost mesmerized. "But I have a request."

"Anything," he said without breaking eye contact. Was there any chance he felt the same way she did?

Could she ask for what she wanted straight out?

He gave a look that urged her to continue. So, she did.

"This might seem like it's out of the blue but..."

Morgan leaned toward her as his gaze dropped to her lips.

"Would you mind kissing me?"

8

Morgan didn't need a whole lot of encouragement to fulfill Avril's request. Since there wasn't a whole lot of distance between them anyway, he leaned in until his lips met hers. She tasted like dark roast coffee as his mouth moved against hers. Dark roast was his new favorite taste.

Before things could get out of hand, he pulled back enough to rest his forehead against hers. The kiss had barely started but held the promise of destroying every kiss up to this point and every one after.

Damn.

"I should probably make something to eat," he said, hearing the gravel-like quality to his own voice. He cleared his throat to ease the sudden dryness in his mouth and tried to regain his normal tone as he sat up.

"I'm not sure I could—"

"Will you at least try?" he asked, cutting her off. "You've been through a lot and there's more track in front of us. You need to stay strong and a big part of that is eating."

She relented with a nod. "A shower would be nice, and a

change of clothes. But the last part is probably asking too much."

"I can throw yours in the wash while you shower," he said, the gravel-quality returned in full force. The last thing he needed was to be thinking about Avril naked in his shower. His voice was already giving him away. "I have one of those fifteen-minute washers. Patience isn't my strong suit. The dryer is just as fast."

"Wow," she said. "I had no idea they even made those."

He smiled. "I can give you a robe to wear once you're out of the shower."

"Okay," she said, leaning back in her chair like she needed to be as far away from him as possible. Did she regret asking for the kiss?

"I'll just grab a robe," he said, excusing himself. He walked into the master and retrieved one he'd gotten for Christmas from his aunt years ago. It hung in his bathroom even though he never once used the cotton bathrobe. "Here you go." He handed the royal blue cover over after making his way back into the kitchen area. Aunt Lucia had embroidered his name on the breast pocket. The woman and his mother couldn't be more opposite. Aunt Lucia was home and hearth, whereas his mother was glitz and glam. It was no wonder the two of them never became close, despite living on the same land for decades.

There was a story behind his mother and father's courtship, or so Morgan had been told. Maybe one of these days he'd ask his father about the past. Was it too much to hope there were good memories buried back there?

"Thank you," Avril said after taking the offering. She excused herself to the guest bathroom. The cabin only had two bedrooms. The third room had been turned into an office. And there were two and a half baths.

Morgan turned around and walked to the fridge, so he wouldn't watch Avril leave the room. There were eggs and bacon in the fridge. He didn't have any leftovers of his aunt's famous meatballs, but those weren't breakfast food. They were good enough to eat twenty-four hours a day as far as he was concerned. But others might not see it the same.

He could whip up a decent omelet, throw in enough vegetables to give the dish some teeth. There was fruit and yogurt in case Avril couldn't eat much. That would give her something to nibble on.

Her determination to keep going without sleep would catch up to her at some point, and she would need to sleep. Speaking of whom, she returned wearing nothing but his robe. Her balled up clothing was in her hands.

"I can throw these in if you point me in a direction," she said. The flush in her cheeks only made her more beautiful.

"It's no trouble," he said, taking the wad of clothes. Hell, he could use a shower after breakfast before they got started on the day. Maybe he could convince her to squeeze in another nap either here or on the road.

"Are you sure?" she asked. "Doing my laundry was never part of the bargain."

"It's one of my many talents," he quipped, trying to lighten the mood.

"Really?"

"No," he said with a chuckle. "But I'm glad you thought it was possible."

Avril smiled, and it was like the sun came out after weeks-long clouds. "Okay, wise guy. I'll leave you to it."

"You should find all the supplies you need in the cabinet or in a drawer," he said. "The towels hanging are for guests." Not that he had a whole lot of those. At least, none that stayed the night. He'd been content with occasional untethered companionship with women who wanted the same. Call him a serial monogamist, except without the emotional attachment part. That, he could do without.

Although, he could admit there was an emptiness to his life recently. Was it because so many of his family members had found real love? Having grown up with Jackie and Keifer for parents, Morgan had never been convinced real love existed. Even Aunt Lucia and Uncle Brody had a twisted relationship. Uncle Brody used to treat her something awful. He would never understand why a good person like her stayed in a bad marriage. Recently, they'd worked through their differences and Uncle Brody seemed to wake up to the amazing woman who'd stood by his side—for far too long in Morgan's opinion. But getting to that point had taken decades.

Not everyone was cut out for long-term relationships. Thinking he was missing out on something would pass once the shine wore off everyone's relationships and the fights began. Although, to be fair, his cousins and siblings seemed to be rock solid in their relationships. Some had children or were planning weddings. It struck him as odd to see them so happy, which only proved how twisted he truly was. What person thought two people being happy was strange?

Which was exactly the reason he never planned to go down that road. But if he ever did, the kiss would have to compare to the brief one he'd shared with Avril a little while ago.

Where did that come from?

Giving himself a mental headshake, he moved into the next room, tossed the clothes in the washer along with detergent, and started the cycle.

Figuring he had time, he hopped in the shower and then brushed his teeth. After throwing on clean clothes, he switched the laundry to the dryer. The fifteen-minute clean cycle truly was one of life's great miracles. Living alone, he'd learned to be self-sufficient a long time ago.

Back in the kitchen, he pulled together ingredients for the omelet and threw some bacon on the griddle on his stove. He'd also learned to do a little basic cooking or starve. He'd never been fond of TV dinners. The portions were too small, so he'd figured his way around a few dishes. They weren't fancy but were enough to keep him from going hungry. He'd grown up with a cook and a housekeeper, which had been awful training for real life. But Jackie Firebrand couldn't be bothered to set foot in the kitchen, unless it was to pour another glass of champagne.

After chopping onions and bell peppers, he cracked open several eggs. He threw all those ingredients into a bowl before grabbing a whisk. He poured a little milk in for good measure and then threw in spinach. The bacon was done on one side by the time the skillet warmed enough to cook on. He poured the ingredients in and then grabbed a spatula.

Bacon crisp and ready, it was time to turn the omelet. He managed a nice half flip.

"That smells amazing," Avril said as she made her way into the kitchen. Her long, wavy hair was wet from the shower. He forced his attention onto breakfast and off the droplet of water rolling down her delicate neck. She had a rare mix of strength and vulnerability. She had a graceful, elegant air that said she could hold her own in a conversation. And she had the intelligence to back it up.

Avril Capri was the total package. If he met someone like her under different circumstances, he might reconsider his position on long-term relationships.

"Almost done," he said.

"What can I do to help?" she asked.

"Plates are in the cupboard," he said, motioning toward the one closest to the fridge.

"Got em," she said, heading over while holding onto the bathrobe with the kind of grip meant for walking tightropes. She retrieved the plates, located silverware, and set the table as he pulled the bacon from the griddle and cut off the stovetop.

He plated the meal and then poured himself another cup of coffee. "Do you need a refill?"

Avril held her hand out long enough to reveal it trembled. "As much as I'd like to say yes, I probably shouldn't. It doesn't look like my body can handle much more."

"You can have another one later," he said. "No rush."

She sat down and picked up her fork. In a matter of minutes, her plate was clean. "Well, I didn't think I would be able to eat much, but that doesn't seem to be the case. You're a really good cook."

"I'll take the compliment," he said with a self-satisfied smile. "Can't say that I know how to cook a whole lot of dishes, but I'm decent at what I know how to do."

Morgan felt it. The slide down the slippery slope that led to having real feelings for Avril Capri. There was something about the way she smiled, despite not doing it nearly enough, that made the weight of the world he carried on his shoulders seem lighter, bearable. One look was all it took for an ache to form in his chest, an ache that made him want to kiss her again.

The question was whether or not he could stop it.

∾

AVRIL NEEDED A DISTRACTION. Having a meal with someone

who'd cooked for her shouldn't rank up there with one of the most intimate moments of her life. It did.

Since she'd already messed up the sheriff's investigation, she figured it wouldn't hurt to read some of the comments to mine for clues, if there were any. But first, she needed to earn her keep. She stood up and then cleared the table.

"You don't have to do that," Morgan insisted.

"Yes, I do," she countered. "I already got a free meal out of the deal. Let me do my part."

Morgan shot her a look.

"What?"

"Nothing," he mused. She wanted in on the joke.

"Seriously, what?"

"I'm not used to having someone over, who is as stubborn as I am," he said with a chuckle that was a low rumble in his chest. Morgan had the kind of deep timbre that made her want to stand a little closer as it washed over her and through her.

"It's the only way I know how to get things done," she said, thinking the trait had saved her from giving up so many times when she'd wanted to fold up. Her stubborn streak might be a mile long, but she tried to use it to her advantage. It was the reason she was successful in business. Refusing to give up could be a good quality when applied to the right situations. In her younger days, she'd used it to stay in relationships too long. She'd been a magnet for young guys who needed fixing, and she'd thrown herself into the task. It took years for her to figure out those guys needed a mother, not a girlfriend.

"I didn't say it was necessarily bad," he defended, joining her at the sink.

She swatted at his hand as he reached for a dish, gave a

light tap. "Nope. I said I'm on dish duty. I meant it. You get to sit back while I clean up."

"Okay, boss," he said, taking a seat at the granite island. He pulled his laptop over and studied the screen. Her sister's channel was still up. He played through the last few videos. Hearing the sound of Mazie's voice deepened Avril's resolve to find her sister. Alive.

Yes, alive. It was the only outcome she could let herself imagine. If evidence proved otherwise, she would deal. Right now, hope was the only thing keeping her going no matter how tiny the sliver or how much it was shrinking.

Being with Morgan gave her a sense of calm she knew better than to lean into. And yet, that was exactly what she wanted to do. Even for a short time. She wanted a mental break from everything her life had become.

After placing the last plate in the dishwasher, and then closing the door, she walked straight over to Morgan. "Is it a bad idea for me to kiss you again?"

He looked over at her where she stood, and then swiveled his chair until she could step in between his thighs. She dropped her hands to rest on powerful muscles, not the kind gained at the gym on a machine but from hard work. There was something incredibly sexy about a person who put in the work, instead of creating showpieces for ego's sake.

"It's the worst of bad ideas," he finally said before locking gazes. "But I won't let that stop me if you won't."

9

Morgan brought his hands up to cup Avril's face, bringing those pink lips closer to his until they met in the middle. The second her lips touched his, a bomb detonated inside his chest. He teased his tongue inside her mouth, and she matched him stroke for stroke.

Spark turned to wildfire in a matter of seconds.

Avril's hands came up to his shoulders, where her nails dug into his skin. The move sent heat spiraling through him, causing him to deepen the kiss.

As her mouth moved against his, everything else faded into the background. His breathing quickened and his pulse skyrocketed. Her hands felt familiar on him despite knowing her for barely a day. The same sensation struck as when they first met. It was the feeling he'd known her all his life, a sense this person was going to be important to him for reasons he had yet to understand.

Avril stepped between the V his thighs made, bringing her body flush with his.

Morgan was in trouble. If this went much further, he'd

hit the point of no return and would be unable to stop himself. He had about five seconds left before it was too late. So, he pulled on all the willpower he had left to break the kiss.

Both were out of breath, as though they'd sprinted a couple of blocks. But their breathing was in sync. He brought his palm up to the base of her throat where her heart beat rapidly. The rhythm matched his. He'd never been so in line with anyone before.

The realization caught him off guard and threatened to break down his walls. But didn't all people let each other down eventually? Whatever was simmering between the two of them, lust or the real deal, threatened to boil over and burn everything in its path.

Taking in a deep breath, Morgan closed his eyes and willed his pulse to slow down.

"We should probably get back to it," he said, hearing that same gravelly quality to his voice. Avril had an effect on him like none he'd ever experienced. He needed to wrap his mind around how and why this was so different. *She* was so different. And why this difference threatened to blow up his world as he knew it.

"Right," she said, biting her bottom lip as he opened his eyes. "That was..."

"A lot," he supplied when she didn't seem able to find the words."

"I was going to say, 'good.'"

He feigned offense. "I'd like to think I was better than that."

Avril laughed, and it broke some of the sexual tension that had corded every last one of his muscles. They'd been strung so tight he thought they might snap.

"It was better than good," she said quietly as a red blush crawled up her neck.

Morgan had to shake off his physical reaction to her or he'd never get anything accomplished today. At least Nick had stopped by and could spread the word that Morgan wasn't available to work today. He could count on his twin to have his back.

Who did Avril have?

"Let's check the screen," he said, redirecting. The way her eyes became glittery with something that looked a whole lot like need wasn't helping. He slapped up the only boundary he could, physical space between them. "On second thought, you do that while I take a walk."

Going outside and getting fresh air always helped clear his mind.

"You sure?" she asked, clearly confused by the shift in direction.

"Yep," he confirmed after toeing on his boots. "I won't go far."

His reassurance resonated. The tension lines in her face smoothed and her shoulders relaxed. She nodded.

"I'll see if there's anything here worth checking out," she said, nodding toward the laptop screen.

"Sounds good," he said, realizing they'd bounced around the word 'good' more times in the past couple of minutes than he had the month preceding it.

Morgan walked outside into a late morning sun, and quickly surveyed the area. A cold front had whipped through recently but today was warm and sunny. He tilted his face toward the sky, enjoying the warmth on his skin.

It occurred to him someone could be out in the thicket, watching. The person who'd run Avril off the road might be nearby. The bastard had found her on the highway heading to her motel. Speaking of which, they should probably grab her things and get her checked out since she planned to stay with him.

Outside, he could think. He could breathe. Being on the land that was just as much part of his soul as his skin was a part of his body had a grounding effect.

Deciding against a walk, he peeked inside the cabin. "Want to check out of your motel?"

Avril bit down on her bottom lip and her forehead creased, a sure sign she was conflicted.

"The bastard who followed you might know where you're staying," he explained.

"It would be nice to have my own toothbrush and more clothes than what's on my back," she finally said after a thoughtful pause. Had she been considering leaving altogether?

"I'm assuming you want to stay here with me," he said, feeling around to see where her head was at.

"I thought about going home just now," she admitted. "If I wasn't still freaked out by the highway incident and without transportation, I would just head there. It might be better to be closer to Austin, since the only reason I came out here was to poke around about you."

The reasoning made sense and yet he didn't want her to leave. No one in or around Austin had her back. "You're welcome to stay here as long as you like."

"Thank you," she said. Then, she issued a sharp sigh. "I'm at a loss right now. I'm trying to filter through all these comments, but the sheriff is right. I kicked up a dust storm. My eyes are crossing trying to read all these. Most think this is some kind of contest, and they have to guess her location to win money."

"The thought of money is probably flooding the site.

The good news is the sheriff has someone on it too," he said. "I'm sure they'll be able to sift through the comments faster and with a skilled eye to ferret out real leads."

Avril issued a sharp sigh. "I just hope that I haven't made it more complicated to find her."

"You stirred up the pot," he said. "That's not necessarily a bad thing."

"I hope you're right," she admitted. "That also has me thinking it might not hurt to take a break and clear my belongings out of the motel, since I'm not going back there. Afterward, I have to think about getting a rental car from my insurance company, which I haven't even called yet. I should have made contact right away, but my head isn't in the right place to handle the details. I don't know why I didn't think about it before."

Because her life had been on the line. She'd been caught off guard and was probably still trying to process what had happened.

"You don't have to deal with any of this," he reassured. "I had your car towed after the sheriff was done collecting evidence and investigating the scene. It's being looked at for repairs or whether it needs to be totaled as we speak."

"When did you do all that?" she asked in shock.

"You'd be surprised what you can accomplish on these smartphones via voice command while driving," he said.

Avril stood up and grabbed her purse. "No word from the sheriff since we last spoke, by the way."

"I'm not surprised," he said. "None of the neighbors remember anyone and our last conversation with him wasn't long ago." Patience wasn't something he'd ever excelled at in his youth. With age, he was improving. Impatience and a stubborn streak had never been the best combination. He'd gone off half-cocked and then been too stubborn to back down when he'd crossed lines he knew better than to cross.

Maturity helped with perspective. Age helped cure the stupidity that came with being immature.

He walked inside, locking the door behind him. After grabbing his phone, wallet, and keys, he led the way to the garage. Halfway there, he reached for Avril's hand, then linked their fingers.

After opening the passenger door, he rounded the front of the vehicle to the driver's side before claiming the seat. He took the full thirty minutes to drive to the hotel, watching out for any signs of an interested driver in a truck in the rearview.

The motel lot had a dotting of vehicles parked.

"I'm in number 12," Avril said after digging around in her purse and then producing a physical key.

The motel had been around since the dawn of time. The owners had a reputation for keeping clean rooms.

The tiny hairs on the back of his neck pricked. It was the same feeling he got when he was being watched.

∽

As Morgan exited the truck, an ominous feeling settled over her. "Do you feel like we're being watched?"

Morgan surveyed the lot, stayed quiet. He kept the door open and placed himself in between her and the possibility of danger. "I have the same feeling, but I don't see anyone." He kept his back to her as he placed his feet in an athletic stance, three feet apart. His hands fisted at his sides. "Do you want to call the sheriff for an escort?"

She gave it a little thought and decided against it. "That shouldn't be necessary. It's just a feeling, and we're probably both on high alert anyway after everything that's happened. Plus, we can get in and out in a matter of minutes. My suitcase is sitting open on the bed and it'll take two seconds to grab my makeup bag and toiletries. Plus, it could take him a long time to get here and he might even be grabbing a few hours of sleep after being up all night."

Her racing pulse tried to convince her body it needed to be on full alert. She took in a deep breath as Morgan finished scrutinizing the dotting of parked cars.

"Key in hand?" he asked.

"Yes, it is," she said, making sure the jagged edge of the key stuck out between her index and middle finger as she fisted her hand. She might not be as strong as someone like Morgan, but she was resourceful. She could only hope it would tip the scale in a fight if it came down to blows with someone.

"Let's go," he said.

It didn't go unnoticed by Avril that he continued to position his body between her and possible danger as he shifted to walking behind her. He placed his hand on the small of her back, which felt strangely intimate under the circumstances.

She was still kicking herself for being run off the road, but she'd never studied evasive procedures. Never realized she might need them. All her training was focused on hand-to-hand self-defense. Using physics against someone by leaning into the back of their knee and then twisting to bring an opponent down.

Avril made a beeline toward her room, slid the key into the lock after a couple of attempts, and opened the door. Her shaky hands were no help.

The room had a pair of double beds. The theme of the room was flowers. There were spring flowers on the bedspreads, along with matching curtains. The thick-piled carpet was the color of grass.

The place was simple, clean, and got the job done. Avril hadn't planned on being here longer than she needed to be. The bed looked comfortable despite never having spent the night here. She'd been too eager to check out Morgan Firebrand and locate her sister.

Inside, nothing looked different on the surface. But she could have sworn that she put out her pajamas.

"What's wrong?" Morgan asked after taking one look at her.

"Something's off."

10

Morgan tensed. He held a hand up to stop Avril from taking another step inside. He closed and locked the door behind them as she took a step back, and then wrapped her fingers around a lamp. Good.

Slowly, quietly, he moved through the small space. There was a bathroom door that was ajar on the left. Directly in front of him was a dressing area complete with sink and mirror. And then there was another door. Closet? It was the only thing that made sense.

They'd already made a lot of noise, so the jig was up if someone was here. But the bastard didn't know exactly when they would strike. He could feel Avril right behind him. She moved stealth-like.

The closet door came first. But this close, he checked the mirror where he could see a sliver into the room. The bathroom light was off. Thankfully, the curtains were drawn despite the daylight hour.

He studied the mirror to see if anything moved inside the darkness. Nothing.

It didn't mean no one was there.

Morgan eased another step forward, slowly bringing his hand up to the door. In one motion, he pushed the door open and flipped on the light. The shower curtain was shoved to one side, the room empty.

He took a step backward and then opened the closet door. It was empty as well.

"Someone was in here," Avril said after a slow exhale.

"What makes you think so?" he asked.

"My clothes," she said. "I know that I set my pajamas out and now they're inside the suitcase. It's all neat, which is how I left it. But the clothes are back inside my suitcase."

"Are you thinking someone didn't want you to notice they were here?" he asked.

"It's the only thing that makes sense," she said as she walked over to the second bed and then sat on the edge. "You don't think the sheriff would come rooting around in my things, do you?"

He shook his head. "Lawler would have done things right, but I can't speak for Austin PD. We can ask the manager to be sure."

"What about the maid?" she asked.

"Did you sleep here?" he asked.

"No," she said.

"Housekeeping could be responsible," he admitted.

She turned toward her suitcase and pulled out the top layers of folded clothing. "Nothing appears to be missing, so that's good."

"Someone might have been looking for information about you," he said. "Trying to see what they could dig up."

"When did your sister contact you, by the way?" he asked, realizing he hadn't asked. "After how many dates?"

"The first one," she supplied. "Why?"

"Because if someone used my likeness to talk her into a date, wouldn't she have known I didn't show up?" he asked. "Does that make sense?"

"Actually, it does," she said.

"Maybe we should be digging deeper into her interactions," he said.

"I requested the information from the app, and never heard back," she said. "They have a 'contact' link on the site, but no one ever got back to me."

"Figures," he said. "I wonder if the sheriff is going down that trail?"

"He might be," she said. "He did say that he had a tech person checking out my sister's site, so it stands to reason the person would also check the dating site where allowed by the law."

He nodded. "The timing is off to me."

"I know what you mean now that I really think about it." Avril set the clothes down. "She goes on one date and calls me to say she's met the one. This guy is different. Although, to be fair, that wasn't the first time I'd heard those words come out of her mouth."

"She was going on the second date and then disappeared without a trace," he said, confirming what he thought he knew so far.

"No, she disappeared after making contact with me to tell me about the first date," she said. "I can't confirm there was a second date because the phone call lasted two seconds."

"Either I've got a doppelganger walking around out there somewhere who isn't my brother, or there's more foul play than we suspected," he stated. "Did you see your sister or was the conversation over the phone?"

"Come to think of it, she texted," she said after a

thoughtful pause. "Did I say we spoke in person before? Because if that's the case, the sheriff could be barking up the wrong tree in his investigation. Following the wrong trail."

"Lawler is probably looking at this from every angle," he said.

The sound of a car engine outside caused Avril to stand up. She tossed clothes inside the suitcase and grabbed her makeup bag and toiletries before setting them inside and zipping the overnight bag. "We should go."

Morgan walked over to the window and peeked outside. A couple walked, hand-in-hand toward the office. He highly doubted those two would even notice if he and Avril stepped outside. The two seemed only to have eyes for each other. "Do you need to check out?"

"Not in person," she said. "I can make a call. Besides, I will have already been charged for today since checkout was at eleven a.m. Technically, I have this place until tomorrow."

"Might not be bad to see if anyone shows up asking for you, thinking you might still be here," he said. "The front desk should be able to tell you when you call to check out if you wait until tomorrow."

"Right," she said on a sigh. "I didn't think about that before. This is all so strange because I teach people how to physically defend themselves from an attack, but this is on a whole new level. Plus, a lot of good my defense lessons did my sister."

"You don't know what impact you have on someone until much later," he said, hearing the guilt in her voice. He reached for her suitcase handle, brushing her hand in the process. Skin-to-skin contact was a bad idea, even if only briefly. The electrical current sizzled, running up his arm, causing a shock to the place he could least afford it, his heart.

After exiting the building, he deposited the overnight bag behind the back seat of his truck. "I can run the key to the drop box. I doubt anyone will check this until later or tomorrow morning."

"Mind if I go with you?" she asked. "I just don't want to be out of reach."

"Sure," he said, taking the key and experiencing more of that electric shock. It made him think of the few kisses they'd shared and how much promise they'd held. Right now wasn't the time to go down that path, though.

He glanced around the lot to make sure no new cars were present. And then jogged over to the key return box. After dropping it inside, he reached for Avril's hand, linking their fingers, before jogging back to the truck.

She took the passenger side and he claimed the driver's side. Neither one wasted time.

She rattled off her address, which he entered into his phone's navigation system before heading out of the parking lot.

"I'll text Lawler to see if he's checked into my sister's dating app," she said, reaching inside her purse. She fired off the message before setting her phone on her lap. Pinching the bridge of her nose like she was staving off a headache, she said, "Are you hungry?"

It was a good sign she was.

"I could eat," he admitted. He could also go a long time without, and often had to remind himself to eat while out on the land. "I have power bars in a supply bag tucked behind my seat for those times I'm out too late and can't get back to the house fast enough. Think that'll hold you over until we reach your place?"

"It should be fine," she said. "I always get headaches

when I need to eat. My stomach isn't convinced food is a good idea, but I can feel my blood sugar dropping."

"Help yourself to as much as you want," he said, motioning toward the back. "We can stop off once we get on the highway if that's not enough."

As she reached over the seat, her cell buzzed. She glanced over after checking the screen. "It's from the sheriff. My sister's profile was deactivated two hours ago."

∼

AVRIL COULD SCARCELY BREATHE. "This can't be a good sign."

"Ask if he knows if the owner of the site deactivated it for her or if it happened from a user standpoint," Morgan insisted with a measured calm in his voice.

She typed in the question.

Those three dots indicating he was typing back sat there for what felt like eternity but was a matter of seconds. Then came, *checking into it.*

"He doesn't know," she said to Morgan, trying not to let her mind jump to all kinds of bad conclusions "Said he's trying to find out."

Could someone have set up the account in the first place to throw law enforcement off? Did that even make sense? Why would someone do that? She understood implicating a person by setting up a fake profile on one end. But setting it up on both didn't exactly scan for her.

Which left her fearing someone knew Mazie wasn't coming home.

The thought gutted Avril. Hunger was no longer an issue. She couldn't get a bite down if she tried. As it was, acid burned the back of her throat. Her worst fear gripped her.

Avril smacked her palm on the hand rest. The move shocked her brain out of the spiral it had been in.

"We'll figure this out together," Morgan's calm voice broke through her heavy thoughts.

For the first time in her life, she didn't feel alone. Despite knowing her mother had loved her as best as she could, Avril had always carried the burden of taking care of things around the house, while her mother worked extra jobs to make ends meet. She woke up early on the weekends and shopped yard sales to find things to resell. She would embellish jackets and then stick a higher price on them, sometimes selling them at consignment shops instead of having her own sales. She took pictures and posted them on coffee shop and grocery store bulletin boards, in addition to working a regular job as a preschool teacher. Her mother depended on her to look after Mazie, cook, and clean.

At a young age, Avril basically took care of the small apartment where they lived. She saw to it her younger sister had a lunch and made it to the school bus until she moved out on her own to go to school. Mazie had mentioned feeling abandoned by Avril in those days. The subject was touchy, and she didn't bring it up often.

And then her mother delivered the devastating news. At first, Avril couldn't believe it was true. Her mind decided one of the three-year-olds in her mother's class must have passed along a virus that mimicked the terminal diagnosis. Avril decided the doctors had it wrong despite the evidence her mother showed. She'd gone with her mother to appointments and then tried to show a brave face when her mother would break down.

That was the worst. Seeing her mother—a mother Avril had always believed could survive anything—fall apart. She'd had no one to lean on, except her girls. At least, that's what she would say. There were no grandparents, no aunts or uncles. Her mother didn't trust anyone on their father's side. He'd been the most responsible one, and look how that had turned out. Not good. As it turned out, his devotion had an expiration date. He'd spiraled and gone back to partying, stating he wasn't ready for a family after their second child was born. He was behind on child support and unemployed, so his brother talked him into robbing a convenience store.

Avril lost track of the man during his first jail term. For all she knew, he was still there or back there. Didn't know. Didn't care.

In some cases, walking away from family and never looking back was the best course of action. Her mother had taught her that lesson and allowed her a peek into her former in-laws' activities. Most were in and out of jail for small crimes, using the penal institutions like a revolving door.

There'd been no way in hell Avril would have reached out to any of those family members. It wouldn't have mattered anyway. No judge in their right mind would have allowed them to take Mazie. The foster care system had been her best bet in the court's eyes.

Guilt slammed into her once again for not being there to protect Mazie.

"She's a grown woman now," Morgan said as though he could read her thoughts. "You get quiet when you're blaming yourself. And you bite down on your bottom lip." He kept his gaze on the stretch of road ahead of them as cars weaved in and out. They were getting closer to the city. It was obvious based on traffic. "Your forehead creases too."

"Is it weird that I'll always think of her as little Mazie? The girl who screamed and cried for me as I had to help the social worker get her into the backseat of the car? Her face will be burned into my memories. Even now, when I know she's an adult, I can't shake that face."

"Hell, I feel protective of my younger-by-two-minutes twin brother Nick," he stated. "We used to torture each other as kids, but no one else could pick on him."

"I guess being and feeling like the older sibling never goes away," she said. "We're always going to want to take care of them."

"Not me," he said with a chuckle. "Not with Nick. He's way too grown for me to worry about."

His laugh was a low rumble in his chest. It broke up some of the stress she'd been feeling on the drive.

"You already know what's going on with my mother," he said. "Now *that* I feel responsible for."

"When my mother was sick, I felt so much guilt for not being with her all the time before the diagnosis," she admitted.

"So, you understand on some level parental guilt as well," he said. "I'm having a hard time shaking that one even though I had nothing to do with her actions."

"I was about to tell you that none of that was your fault and you shouldn't blame yourself, but that would make me a first-class hypocrite," she admitted. "It's so much easier to see a situation clearly when it involves someone else."

He nodded. "Sometimes, it's better to be reminded that someone is a grown woman capable of making her own choices. And that no one is immune to making mistakes."

"She is grown," Avril agreed. "And I shouldn't blame myself for her actions any more than you should blame yourself for what your mother did."

"Doesn't mean we won't, though."

There was a lot of truth to his statement. Was carrying the guilt a large part of the reason she didn't have room for much else?

11

Morgan parked in front of 1234 Park Street. The bungalow-style home sat on the corner of a small subdivision north of Austin city limits. The house was five minutes off the highway and sat on a small parcel of flat land. The Hill Country was farther south.

"Home sweet home," Avril said on a sigh. Was she dreading going inside? "You don't think someone could have gone through my home, do you? I know I mentioned it last night but I'm hopeful that was fear talking."

"Do you keep the doors locked?" he asked.

She shot him a surprised look at the question. "Doesn't everyone?"

"Not where I'm from," he said. "At least, not until recently."

"I can't even imagine having that kind of freedom," she said. "I've grown up in and around a larger city, so it's more surprising that I don't have an alarm system already installed."

"We can walk the perimeter before going inside," he said. "Check for any signs of a break-in."

"That's a good idea," she said. "I was just thinking the same thing."

The bungalow had a small yard that was enclosed with a chain-link fence. The landscaping looked to have native plants, good for conserving water.

He started for the door handle but stopped short after glancing over at Avril. "We can go grab a bite to eat if you're not ready to go inside."

It was getting late and the power bar he'd eventually convinced her to eat couldn't possibly be holding her.

"I have food inside," she said with a renewed determination in her voice. "I'm not much in the kitchen, but I've managed to survive this long on what I know how to cook."

"Okay," he said before exiting the truck. He kept a close eye out for any movement as he rounded the front, and then opened the door for Avril. She took the hand he offered as more of that now-familiar shock rocketed up his arm and then exploded in the center of his chest. All he could do at this point was grin. It had been too long since anyone had affected him this way. Rather than fight against it, he decided to lean into it. After all, their interactions were sure to be short-lived. Once they found her sister and cleared his name once and for all, he would go back to ranch life and she would return here.

Would life without her ever be the same?

Morgan gave himself a mental headshake. Contemplating a future with anyone, let alone Avril was as productive as trying to get honey from a cow. Cows gave milk. It was all they were capable of giving. His upbringing would always cause him to put the brakes on when he got too close to someone.

He didn't do relationships and he didn't do long-term. Period.

If he needed a reason, he only had to look at his own parents. They'd believed they were in love once. Didn't they? Or, looking back, had his mother been nothing more than a trophy wife? It would be just like his father to marry the prettiest girl in order to one-up his brother. Morgan's grandfather had always pitted his two sons against each other. Competition, he'd preached, caused the cream to rise to the top.

Morgan had news for his grandfather. Cream would have floated to the top anyway. Competition among family members destroyed relationships.

He reached for Avril's hand at the same time she reached for his. He linked their fingers as they walked side-by-side, letting go briefly to open the gate.

The first stop was an obvious place, the front door. There were no signs of the lock being jimmied or the wood being broken. Twisting the handle, the door was still locked. He moved to the windows next, checking each one as they made a circle around the house. The home itself was painted a light beige color. The garage door, front door, and a couple of accents were painted steel blue.

Steadily, stealthily, they worked their way around the home. When it was deemed safe, she unlocked the door and they moved inside.

The interior was as simple and warm as the outside. White-washed wood floors covered the living room, dining room, and kitchen space, all of which was open concept. An oversized linen-covered sofa faced a fireplace that had a flatscreen TV mounted above it. The brick on the hearth was painted to match the exterior, using a slightly lighter shade of beige. A dining room had a round table built for two. The art on the walls was simple and added warm colors to the light walls. All-in-all, there was enough of a feminine touch to make the place feel soft and comfortable, a place where he could see himself spending a lot of time.

"Do you have a studio here?" he asked.

"It's in the second bedroom," she said. "There are only two and I didn't want to feel like I lived at work, so I set up in the spare bedroom. It's small, but it works. Plus, I have the added benefit of being able to close the door to feel like my work is done for the day."

"Not a problem for my line of work," he said with a chuckle as he walked toward the hallway he presumed led to the bedrooms. "Makes sense though."

After clearing both and a hall bathroom, he joined Avril in the kitchen, where she rummaged through the fridge.

"I may have overestimated my fridge contents," she said, pulling out a to-go box of leftovers. Her nose wrinkled after one sniff and the whole box ended up in the trash. She grabbed her phone and studied the screen. "What sounds good? Tex-Mex? Italian?" She paused. "Although, the Italian place has new owners, so maybe not that one. They're not as good as they used to be."

"Is that one of those food delivery apps?" he asked.

She nodded. "What sounds good?"

"Mind if I check the pantry and fridge?" he asked. "I'm guessing we'll eat a whole lot faster that way."

Avril folded her arms across her chest. "Be my guest." Then she added, "This should be good."

He walked over and checked out the contents. The fridge had several tins of leftovers. He checked a few, found one with chicken that looked salvageable from a Chinese dish. He grabbed a couple of green onions that hadn't completely wilted. There was a can of mixed veggies in the pantry, along with rice.

After locating a decent-sized stir fry pan, he drained the water out of the veggies and then boiled water for the boil-in-bag rice.

"Do you have soy sauce?" he asked.

She frowned. "No. I'm afraid I order out more than I cook." And then an idea dawned. "But wait, I have packets." She moved to a drawer next to the silverware and produced a handful. "Look here."

He smiled and took them. Cooking for her gave him more pleasure than he should probably let it. Not to mention the fact he'd never considered himself a whiz. Living on a ranch made him self-sufficient.

Fifteen minutes later, he had two full plates of chicken fried rice.

"I'm impressed," she said as she grabbed a couple of glasses and filled them with water. She brought them over to the table along with a pair of forks. "I thought you said you couldn't cook."

"You'd be surprised at what you can learn when there's no delivery service to make food magically show up at the door," he teased.

"Touché," she fired back, with a smile that could clear up clouds during a Texas thunderstorm.

He ignored the shot to his heart as he set the plates down and then took a seat. "I've had to learn to take care of myself. I had a mother who drank champagne during dinner rather than cook or eat. And then there are times when I'm out hunting down poachers and have to figure out a meal from what I can catch or pick."

"I'm impressed," she admitted, that smile devastating him once more.

Many more shots to the heart like these and there'd be nothing left of him.

⁓

AVRIL KNEW BETTER than to let her guard down very far in Morgan's company. She could get used to having him around and that was a threat to her independence. What good would it do to learn to depend on someone? She'd gotten along fine being her own person, being on her own, and doing life her own way. Why risk it? What good could come of it?

"Once again, you have to let me do the dishes," she said, standing up from the table. Sitting there much longer might make her feel like they were a couple. They weren't. No matter how much she thought about the kisses they'd shared and how every kiss from here on out would be measured against them. Or how they made her feel inside like a fireworks show was going off inside her ribs. Or how weak and rubbery they made her legs as though her bones had melted under the heat.

"I know when I've lost an argument," he said, throwing his hands up to surrender.

Avril shifted her attention to the task at hand. There was something comforting about doing a mundane chore after a chain of stressful events. It grounded her and brought her back to reality. Dishes needed to be washed. It made her feel normal again after her stress levels had been through the roof. It reminded her that life went on. There was comfort in the thought.

As she focused on rinsing each dish and then placing them in the dishwasher, she reminded herself to breathe. In that moment, it seemed like the world wasn't completely falling apart. It felt like things might work out okay and that she could get through this.

Avril closed up the dishwasher. She didn't need to turn around to know that Morgan was standing right behind her. She could feel his presence before breathing in his unique masculine scent.

Rather than step closer and torture herself by not being able to touch him, she got the heck out of there. Her glass of water sat on the table and it seemed like a good idea to take a drink since her throat suddenly dried up.

Reality smacked hard when she glanced at her cell and remembered the message from the sheriff. *Where are you, Mazie?*

If only there was a hint or some clue to follow. As it was, the trail had gone cold. She picked up her phone, pulled up her sister's channel and scrolled. Forty thousand six hundred messages and counting. She watched as messages popped up.

Most folks were expressing concern for Trix, wondering where she'd been. Others were offering tips on where Trix had supposedly been seen last. There were a few conspiracy theorists saying the government picked her up because her channel was getting too popular. Those folks decided politics was to blame for her disappearance. And then, of course, there was a smattering of alien abduction type comments. If only Mazie had been taken to another planet where she was safe and being treated like a queen.

Avril would love to believe commenter *theyrwatching00*.

Reading these, she also realized how loved her sister was for bringing entertainment to so many. The comments about her bringing a smile to someone's face while they were dealing with the death of a loved one or while on chemo filled Avril's heart. It was a beautiful thing that her sister was making contributions to so many people's happiness, especially when they needed it most.

This was all Mazie. She might be a decade younger than Avril, but twenty-three was old enough to know what she wanted in life and go after it. Pride filled her chest as a few rogue tears welled before running down her cheek.

"What is it?" Morgan asked, walking over with a concerned look on his face.

"I didn't realize how much of an impact my sister has on people," she said, using two fingers to push the cell toward him so he would stop before his scent filled her senses again. Too late. He came all the way over and then bent down to check out the screen. Breathing him in wasn't helping with the whole keeping-him-at-arm's-length bit or dimming the wildfire attraction that was simmering underneath the surface.

The fact he probably didn't feel the same helped, despite being certain she could feel electricity crackling in the air between them. Even if there was an attraction on his side, it didn't mean he wanted to pursue a relationship.

A relationship? Where did that even come from?

Avril was under too much duress and the cracks were starting to show. First of all, she wouldn't even consider dating anyone seriously at this point in her life, even if she wasn't searching for her sister. Which brought her to her next point. She was a horrible older sister. Sure, she loved Mazie and checked in on her but that wasn't the same as being responsible for her. And Avril hadn't been able to protect her sister on any front. Her many failures in that department came to mind. Take, for instance, the time Mazie asked twenty-year-old Avril to speak to her teacher. Turned out Mazie was failing math. The district had adopted a new method for teaching math, and it was awful.

Mazie couldn't get the hang of it despite being a decent student. After losing her mother and living in foster care, her grades had dropped. The new math was kicking her little sister's butt.

Going in to have a meeting with the teacher hadn't done a bit of good. Mazie had failed the next test and the next. Avril met her sister after school to help her when she could, but that was spotty because of an unpredictable work schedule. Mazie finally eked out a passing grade but Avril had been reminded how clueless she was when it came to taking care of her sister.

"You're doing that thing again," Morgan said, motioning toward her forehead. "What's on your mind?"

"Nothing," she said, dismissively. She did want to talk to him about it. He was easy to talk to. But getting closer wasn't going to help her when they walked away in a few hours or days, however long it took to find Mazie.

"It can't be nothing," he said. "Your forehead wrinkle doesn't lie."

She could share a little without going down the feelings rabbit hole. "Okay, you got me. I was just remembering how little help I've been to her. Case in point, I couldn't even help her pass math when she was ten years old."

"How old were you at the time?" he asked.

"Twenty," she supplied.

"Wasn't there a big stink about changing up the way kids learned math years ago?" he asked. "It got so much attention, it was all anyone could talk about at the post office or the diner. You know it had to be big for me to know anything about it."

"Yes, but still," she said.

"I don't think many kids were passing math back then," he supplied.

"That might be dramatic," she insisted. "I'm sure *some* kids were."

"Either way, the school system is to blame for adopting a new way to learn without vetting it first," he said. "Plus, what were you doing back then? Working?"

"Yes," she admitted. "Two jobs while going to community college to become a nurse, which lasted all of three semesters."

He shook his head. "I'd ask you if you're always this hard on yourself, but I think I already know the answer."

She playfully tapped him on the shoulder. "What's that supposed to mean?"

"Just that you carry the weight of the world on your shoulders," he clarified, feigning injury.

"Do I?" she asked, thinking out loud.

"I don't have to think too hard on that answer," he pointed out. "Yes."

"You barely know me," she said. "And, let's face it, the conditions under which we've gotten to know what little we know about each other have been extreme."

"Doesn't mean it's not true," he said, standing up straight.

She missed his warmth the second he moved across the kitchen, stopping at the counter where he leaned his hip. Him being across the room was the equivalent of clouds covering the sun. He also had a point. One that resonated.

"I may or may not take responsibility for things that aren't under my control," she finally admitted on a slow sigh.

"Acknowledging you have a problem is the first step toward fixing it," he said with a dry crack of a smile.

"Alright, smarty pants," she quipped, realizing she just

sounded like the old schoolmarm she'd had for a second-grade teacher. She broke into a wide smile.

He did the same in a show of perfectly straight, white teeth.

What could she say? Everything about this man caused her stomach to freefall and an ache to form in her chest. One that made her want to kiss him again.

12

Morgan forced his gaze away from Avril's lips as she spoke. She was temptation multiplied. Right now, what she needed from him was a listening ear. The last thing she needed was for him to try to solve her problems for her. She was an intelligent woman.

Everyone needed someone to bounce ideas off of or to point out their blind spots. Hers was caring too much about things she had no control over. Blaming herself for everything that went wrong. And not being able to give herself a break when she couldn't fix something.

He understood because they were similar in that way. In fact, they may have only known each other for a day and a half, but it felt like they'd known each other their entire lives. The words *kindred spirits* popped into his thoughts again.

"Are you tired yet?" he asked, realizing she hadn't slept in two days. It was long since dark outside and she'd bitten back at least two yawns in the last few minutes alone. "Think you can get some sleep?"

"Here?" she asked, sounding surprised at the idea.

This place was comfortable and it was home for her. He always kept an overnight bag tucked behind his driver's seat for when he got stuck out on the land and couldn't drive back to the house. "Why not?"

"I guess there's no reason we can't," she said. "Since it doesn't look like anyone's been here, it might be safe."

"Doesn't mean no one is watching, but I don't need sleep and if I do, I'm a light sleeper anyway," he said. "Tracking dangerous men hellbent on stealing from your ranch will do that to you."

He also had a Colt .45 in his emergency bag. It did the trick against coyotes and wild hogs who threatened livestock. As much as he hated the idea of killing any living thing, having predators on the land wasn't a risk he could take.

"Okay," she finally said after a thoughtful pause. "It's hard to sleep, you know? Because it feels like wasting time that could be spent searching for her. I have this nightmare every time I close my eyes that I find her a minute too late and she's already gone, but I could have saved her if I'd just gotten there quicker."

"There are more folks looking for her right now than you," he said, trying to ease some of her fears, knowing he could never take them away. "Law enforcement is on your side and they have more resources than we do."

She nodded before tucking her chin to her chest. She shook her head. "Sorry."

When she looked up, a couple of tears broke free and rolled down her cheek. He walked over to her, took a knee, and thumbed them away. "You didn't do anything wrong."

"That thing you said about having the weight of the world on my shoulders is true," she said. "You nailed it. And I have no idea how to make it stop." She paused long enough to take in a fortifying breath. "But when I'm with you, I'm better. I'm not used to someone having my back or having a shoulder to lean on, so this is new territory for me."

She stood up, and he came up right along with her.

"It's good to finally have someone I can count on who won't leave when it gets tough," she said as he looped his arms around her and pulled her closer to him.

"That's not fair," he said, hearing the huskiness in his own voice. It was dangerous to admit but right now he wanted to be the one who was there for her. "You deserve so much more."

She buried her face in his chest, and her quiet sobs ripped his heart to shreds. Her arms wrapped around him and held on like her life depended on it. The fact someone as amazing as her could go through life without anyone watching out for her gutted him. She looked out for her sister and would trade places with her missing sister in a heartbeat if it meant Mazie would be okay.

Avril deserved to have the same and so much more.

Damn, the world could be cruel to all the wrong people. She had a deadbeat father she didn't know anymore. Her mother, who was one of the few good things in her life, died tragically. And now her sister—and only family—was missing.

Anger burned through him as he resolved to see this through, to make certain she was okay no matter what the outcome, and to stay in touch because he wanted to know what was going on in her life. Granted, they couldn't be more opposite. His life was on the ranch. Hers was on the city's fringe. Half the time, he couldn't get decent cell coverage even if he wanted to. But they could meet up for coffee on his day off.

Then again, those would be slim coming up here real

soon once calving season started. His schedule would be out of control for several months on end until early summer. There'd be times when he would be gone for days on end. Being single worked for him. He didn't have to be accountable to anyone else. He could come and go as he pleased. Eat what he wanted when he wanted. He had as much freedom as he wanted. His life was simple. He cooked his own meals and did his own laundry.

Being out on the land was where he felt the most freedom. It had always been that way ever since he was a little kid. The air seemed cleaner even on the hot summer days when most folks couldn't stand to be outside. He was the first one out the door. Always.

Out there, he was as wild as the mustangs that roamed the property. There were no fights between parents that turned into shouting matches. No cruel words being thrown around. No heavy drinking. Out there, his father couldn't raise a hand to smack five-year-old Morgan across the face.

Damn.

This was the first time he recalled that happening. Had he buried the physical abuse down so deep it took thirty years to resurface?

More memories like that one came to light. Now, he was beginning to understand the underlying reason why he rarely ever came indoors when at the ranch. It explained why he was always outside unless made to come in. His parents fought through most of the dinner hour, so the microwave had become his and his brothers' best friend. Morgan was the better cook, and he'd honed his skills while his mother was having her 'relax' time, which basically meant drinking champagne until she passed out. His father spent most of his time trying to get a rise out of Jackie.

No wonder he'd suppressed most of his childhood memories. They weren't worth the effort of remembering.

∽

Avril leaned into Morgan as he whispered sweet reassurances into her ear. He said things like *it'll be alright* and *you're doing better than you think.*

Thinking had never been her problem. Lying awake at night overthinking was a whole different story. She'd been there, done that, got the souvenir.

Was she ready to start a new chapter? To change?

Nothing mattered until she located Mazie, but maybe the time was coming to find a new normal once this was over. Maybe it was time to take care of herself and let others be responsible for their own lives. Maybe she could open her heart a little to an outsider?

The realization struck a chord.

"Thank you," she whispered, not daring to look up. There was no way she could while she was still so vulnerable.

"I didn't do anything yet," he said, his voice low and gravelly.

He had no idea the impact he was having on her, which was probably not a bad thing. After all, she had no plans to continue talking to him once this was over. He was busy. She was busy, or at least would be once her sister was located and brought home.

More of the optimism that had been in short supply surfaced. It was Morgan. He made her feel like everything would magically somehow work out.

"I should probably head to bed," she said, thinking a shower would be nice. "Will you stay with me?"

"I'm here for whatever you need, whenever you need it," he said, pulling back. He tried to make eye contact, but she couldn't manage it. Not now. Not while she was feeling this vulnerable, no matter how safe he made her feel.

"Would you wait for me while I shower?" she asked.

"Let me run out to my truck and grab my overnight bag."

She walked him to the door with her gaze locked onto the wood flooring and then waited as he ran out to retrieve his bag.

This seemed like a good time to make a mental checklist of things she needed to stay safe in the future. The idea of getting a dog sounded pretty good to her right now. She regretted not having an alarm system installed before now. That would come in handy, all things considered. Her sister didn't have one either. A dog would be a nightmare for Mazie, considering the fact she was barely able to take care of herself, but a good security system would add a layer of protection since her building didn't have cameras installed in the hallways.

Avril also realized the best defense was being aware. How many times had she preached that to her followers?

Be aware of your surroundings. It was the first mantra of self-defense.

Making sure no one was around to hurt a person stopped a problem before it happened. Being careful if parked next to a van was another. There were a surprising number of abductions during daylight hours at something as seemingly safe as a grocery store parking lot.

Being educated and aware were the two best weapons for personal safety. After that, a few maneuvers to surprise an attacker and then run away to safety helped.

Morgan jogged back into the house. She locked the door behind him after checking to ensure there were no suspicious vehicles parked on her small street. Once safely inside, she led him to the bedroom.

"I already mentioned there's only one bedroom in use, and I'm hoping you'll stay in here with me while I sleep," she said.

"Go ahead and shower," he urged, something passed behind his eyes. Need? "I'll be here."

Avril decided not to overanalyze why it was so easy to be with Morgan or how fast her heart started beating the second they made eye contact. She decided to take it at face value, grab her pajamas, and head to the bathroom. A quick shower later, and after her teeth were brushed, she exited the bathroom to find him standing in the hallway. His feet here crossed at his ankles as he leaned against the wall and studied his phone.

As far as sexy images went, this one was right up there with the all-time greatest.

"There's a fresh towel on the rack beside mine if you want to take a shower or just freshen up," she said, noticing the gym bag was on the floor next to him.

"I can leave the door open if it makes you feel better," he offered.

"Okay," she said before clearing her throat to ease the sudden dryness at the thought of him being naked and right across the hall.

With that, he bent down and picked up the bag before heading into the bathroom. Since there were two bedrooms and the bathroom sat across the hall in between them, she didn't have a direct line of sight.

Inside her bedroom, she made sure the blinds were completely closed and the curtains drawn. The lamp on her bedside table had several settings. She clicked once for the lowest level of lighting before slipping underneath the covers. She'd grabbed her cell on the way in and was scrolling through comments while the shower water started running across the hall.

Exhaustion caused her eyes to blur and letters to move, so she gave up on the attempt at reading. Besides, her phone needed charging. She set it on the charger and pulled the covers up to her chin. A t-shirt and pajama shorts were her usual go-to clothing for nighttime.

Falling asleep would be impossible, but she could lie there with her eyes closed, resting them until he was done with his shower. This was usually a good state for her. She came up with some of her best ideas in the space between being awake and asleep. This was where she solved problems without even thinking about them. This was a good state.

She rolled over onto her side as the spigot in the bathroom cut off across the hall. Nine-thirty never felt so late. She rarely went to bed before midnight. Sleeping was a whole other story. Most nights, she tossed and turned.

Morgan filled the doorframe. He had on boxers and a white t-shirt. The cotton material stretched across a broad chest, highlighting muscles that went on for days. He motioned toward the chair. "I'll be fine there. Go ahead and get some sleep."

She couldn't let him sleep sitting up in an uncomfortable chair when he was being generous enough to sleep at her place. "Come to bed." Hold on. She heard how that sounded and felt heat rising to her cheeks. "That didn't sound right. What I meant to say is that I trust you, and I'd feel awful if you spent the night in that chair."

He hesitated. For a split second, she thought he might decline the offer. A mix of emotions played out across his face in a matter of seconds, none of which she could pinpoint. Then, he shook his head, cracked a small smile, and joined her in bed. The mattress dipped underneath his weight and, for a split second, she imagined him on top of her, skin-to-bare-naked skin, moving together until the pace became frenzied.

"I checked my phone again," she said. "That was probably a mistake. The post is being viewed as a contest and there's a flood of comments and Trix sightings. It breaks my heart every time someone believes they've seen her because I want it to be true so badly I can scarcely breathe."

"You know how you were giving yourself a hard time about not being a good sister before?" he asked after a long pause.

"Yes," she admitted.

"I'd like to give you my perspective on that," he said.

"Okay."

"Your sister is lucky to have someone who loves her and looks out for her," he started. "Before you point out all the times you believe you let her down, I'd like to remind you of the fact you've stuck it out all these years. Your devotion to her has been unwavering. I'd also like to say no one is perfect at parenting, so becoming a substitute when life hands kids a rough deal. The fact you're still on her side, fighting for her, says a lot about how good of a parent you would be. You love her unconditionally. You've done your best every step of the way."

She started to protest but clamped her mouth shut. His words resonated even though she wasn't quite ready to believe them.

"I don't know much about being a parent," he said. "Based on my experience of having parents, I can tell you that all I needed from them was love and acceptance. You do that for Mazie in spades."

That much was true.

"So, I know you're still going to be hard on yourself because you hold yourself to an almost impossible standard," he continued.

He scored another direct hit.

"And yet, you don't ask anything from anyone else," he continued. "In fact, you go to great lengths to maintain your independence and prove to yourself and everyone around you that you rely on yourself and yourself alone."

She couldn't argue there.

"Anyone would be lucky to have you as a friend," he said. "Because I have a feeling once you love someone, you go deep."

Avril didn't speak up. He'd nailed her to a t, so there was no use fighting it. Could she give herself a break? Could she lighten up? Could she let others in?

Because that felt like the real question here.

Rather than let her defensiveness take the wheel, she stilled and let those words wash through her. He quieted too. The only sound was the beating of his heart, which beat in perfect rhythm with hers.

That was the last sound she heard before falling into a deep sleep.

13

Morgan woke with a start. He didn't dare move as he tried to get his bearings. The soft light made it easier for his eyes to adjust. Avril was sleeping beside him. She'd curled up against him at some point in the middle of the night and her warm body stirred a deep desire inside him. Her steady, even breathing said she was still asleep.

The clock was on the opposite nightstand. He couldn't see it from this side of the bed without disturbing her. Could he reach for his cell without waking her?

The blinds were closed and the curtains drawn, so it was impossible to get a sense of time based on whether or not it was light outside. His internal clock was a mess.

Thankfully, his cell was within reach. He barely twisted his torso to reach it. The time on the screen read seven-thirty. He'd been out for ten hours straight?

No way.

He hadn't slept more than seven consecutive hours since high school. Even at the end of calving season, he went back to his normal pattern rather than binge sleeping. So, it came as a big surprise that he'd been down this long.

He also needed a caffeine boost almost as much as he needed air in his lungs. Getting up quietly would prove a challenge. The thought of disturbing Avril when she was sleeping so soundly didn't seem right. Could he extract himself without waking her?

Did he want to?

The short answer was no, but he needed to check in with Nick and get the day going.

Slowly, he slid out from underneath her arm that had been wrapped around his torso. He instantly missed her warmth. It only took a few more seconds to slip out of bed. The image of the two of them in bed on a Sunday morning, arms and legs twisted in the covers after a night of incredible sex, assaulted him.

He did his level best to shake it off on the way to the bathroom across the hall. His bad breath was far from kissable after a ten-hour nap, and the situation needed to be rectified immediately.

Waking up next to Avril must have put sex on the brain because it wasn't his normal go-to subject before he was even awake. Then again, he couldn't remember the last time he had sex, let alone good sex.

Okay, so he'd mentally said the word sex three times in a row. Time to shift his focus. They weren't any closer to finding Mazie and it frustrated the hell out of him.

That was quite a change in tone, he mused.

Since it was a safer topic than thinking about his growing feelings for Avril, he stayed on it. After brushing his teeth, he headed into the kitchen to make coffee. A quick survey of the pantry and cabinets gave him all the supplies he needed. Since he drank his black, he wasn't worried about whether or not she had fresh milk.

The coffee took less than five minutes to brew a full pot. His cell buzzed as he took the first sip. He'd placed it on the counter while he worked on his caffeine fix. The screen said a call was coming from Nick.

"Hey," Morgan answered. "Everything okay?"

"Remember Spicy Peanut?" Nick said, with a quality in his voice that worried Morgan.

"Everyone's favorite pony?" Morgan asked. "How could I forget? I think we all have a scar somewhere from when the little bugger bit us."

"Yeah," Nick said with a chuckle. "Didn't stop us from loving him though."

"Nope," Morgan agreed. "Or chasing him around the fields forever."

The phone became very quiet.

"Why?" Morgan asked, fearing the worst. "Did something happen?"

"He passed away overnight," Nick stated solemnly.

"Oh no," Morgan stated. "He might be thirty years old, but he was in good health last I checked."

"He must've gotten ahold of something best we can tell," Nick said.

"Like poison?" Morgan asked. "Who would be stupid enough to keep that lying around the barn, where any of the animals could get hold of it?"

"Exactly," Nick agreed. "No one I know. Granted, mistakes can be made but he was healthy before last night."

The beats of silence told Morgan they were most likely thinking the same thing.

"Do you think someone is coming for the family?" Morgan asked.

"Considering what's happening with you, I have questions," Nick said. "Any one of us could be targeted or used as scapegoats because of our mother's actions."

"It might be time to pay a visit to her," Morgan said. "See who else she might have been in league with."

"Or who she might have double-crossed," Nick added.

"True," Morgan said. *Damn.* Losing Spicy Peanut struck him in the center of the chest harder than a physical blow. It was too unexpected to fathom. The pony had been healthy and this was out of the blue.

He told his brother about Mazie's profile being deactivated yesterday. "What do you think it means?"

"You're chasing down a trail from the angle of Mazie right now," Nick said. "Right?"

"I'd like to believe the sheriff is looking at all possibilities, but this one seems to be the most obvious," Morgan supplied.

"We might be a target," Nick confirmed. "I hate to think it's possible, but I'm wondering if Spicy Peanut was killed."

Morgan bit back a few choice words as anger heated the blood in his veins to boiling. It was one thing to target him but to take revenge out on an innocent animal...

He issued a sharp sigh.

"There's a special place in hell for someone who could hurt an animal," he ground out.

"I'd like to be the one to send them there," Nick echoed the same sentiment Morgan was thinking.

"I'll notify Lawler," Morgan said. "He should be in the loop on this."

"I'm not following how Mazie is linked to you," Nick said.

"Me either," Morgan agreed. "That part is a head-scratcher. Plus, she texted her sister after the first date to say she'd met the one."

"Is it possible she was forced to write that text?" Nick asked. "If she made contact with her sister, it would give the bastard more time before anyone started looking for her."

An ominous feeling settled over Morgan. Because it meant the bastard who'd abducted Mazie might have killed her and buried her somewhere on Firebrand property. It would be the best way to seal the deal as far as making it look like Morgan was a murderer.

Nick cursed. "Are you thinking what I'm thinking?"

"Pull as many resources as you can and start looking for a shallow grave on the property," Morgan requested.

"We're on the same page," Nick stated grimly. "I'm on it."

This wasn't the kind of update Morgan wanted to give Avril, but she needed to know.

"Keep me posted," Morgan said to his brother as he grabbed a second coffee cup.

"You know I will," Nick promised. "Watch your back, bro. I can't have anything happening to you."

"You do the same," he said. "And don't forget the two of us look alike. It might be best if you stayed on the ranch until this thing is sorted out."

∼

Avril stretched as she opened her eyes. As she felt around, finding cold sheets instead of Morgan's warm body, she heard his voice in the form of a low hum from down the hall. There was a worried tone even though she couldn't pick out the words.

After quickly freshening up in the bathroom, she headed down the short stretch of hallway. Morgan stood in the kitchen, his back to her and his arms spread out, hands gripping the bullnose edge of the granite counter.

"Who was that?" she asked after clearing her throat so as not to catch him off guard.

"Nick," he said. The tension in his back muscles strung them tight. "Bad news from the ranch. I was just about to wake you."

He gripped two mugs, turned around, and then motioned toward the table. She took a seat as a dark cloud taking over a sunny day feeling took hold.

She looked him straight in the eye. "What is it, Morgan?"

"One of the animals died unexpectedly overnight," he said.

She brought her hand up to cover a gasp. "I'm so sorry."

It was obvious by his demeanor that this animal had been special to him. Then again, he was the kind of person who would see himself as the protector of all things weaker.

"Spicy Peanut," he said, clearly struggling with fighting back emotion. "We got him when Nick and I were five years old and he got his name on day one because he was such a troublemaker."

She reached across the table and touched his hand. He immediately linked their fingers. When he brought his gaze up to meet hers, she saw the mix of hurt and anger. Wished she could do something to take it away or make it better in the way he helped her.

Her heart bled for him, for his pain, and for the frustration in his eyes because he couldn't stop this from happening. She knew the feeling a little too well.

He took in a sharp breath. "I alerted the sheriff to what happened. Between this and the fake profile, we have to take this more seriously. Your family might have been dragged into drama because of mine." He withdrew his hand.

"Because of your mother," she said, echoing what he'd said the other day.

"Yes," he said before dropping his gaze to the rim of his coffee cup. That wasn't a good sign. "Nick is calling all hands on deck as we speak to search as much of the property as possible."

Those words struck like a physical blow.

"Looking for a shallow grave," she said quietly.

"That's right," he said. "If she's there, everyone will do their best to find her."

Avril nodded before standing up.

"I'm the one who is sorry," he said.

She needed to move in order to process, so she paced around the kitchen a couple of times. As much as Morgan might believe the opposite, none of this was his fault. But this wasn't the time to split hairs.

"Can we join the search?" she asked.

"We can do anything you want," he said. "Whatever leads you want to follow, we can do that too."

"Why try to run me off the road?" she asked, mostly thinking out loud.

"Isn't it obvious?" he asked.

The reason dawned on her. "Because I had just left your home. There would likely be DNA evidence when the sheriff came to question you."

"It's the best way to put a nail in my coffin," he said. "Think about it. I meet someone online and she goes missing. The trail leads back to me despite there being no additional evidence of my involvement. Except a body buried on my family's land is a good way to show that I'm the killer. And then you come to question me about your sister after the sheriff picks up the trail. The same night, you go missing."

"There are a lot of holes," she said. "For instance, the lack of communication on cell phone records between you and my sister."

"A body found on my property gets a whole lot of attention from someone sitting in a jury box," he said.

"The burden of proof is on the prosecution," she pointed out. "There's no way they'll convict you of murder without more evidence linking you to the crime."

"A good prosecutor could build a case against me," he said. "My family's image is already tainted from my mother's actions. Not to mention the fact my grandfather didn't exactly have a reputation for being a good person. No, some folks will be too eager to believe we're all rotten apples and lock me away forever."

"But I'm here," she said, hating there could be any truth to those words. In a perfect world, the justice system would work like it was supposed to and jurors wouldn't be tainted. But this was far from a perfect world and people made judgments without all the facts all the time. In recent years, it felt like an even bigger problem. All someone had to do was point a finger to get a celebrity canceled. Proof wasn't always required. Even so, she would like to believe in the good in humanity and that justice was always served despite evidence to the contrary. Politics might be tainted but she prayed the justice system still worked.

"Some folks will convince themselves that I'm just biding my time until I can get rid of you," he said. "They'll think me pitching in to help is all a rouse to throw everyone off, like when a killer shows up to help search for the 'missing' person they know is already dead because they killed them."

She would like to argue but his points were too valid. People snapped to judgment and innocent people went to prison. All anyone had to do was pay attention to the news for confirmation these horrific things happened.

"Give me five minutes to get ready," she said. There was no way she was sitting here when she could be combing the Firebrand property to find her sister. After draining her cup of coffee in a couple of gulps, she headed into her bedroom.

Hair in a ponytail and jeans on, she reemerged to find Morgan with keys in hand and ready to go. He'd managed to throw on clothes while she'd gone into the bathroom and then slipped out without her hearing him.

"I have no idea what we'll find on your family's ranch," she said, horrified at the thought of her sister being buried out in the cold, let alone dead, "but it doesn't make you a killer."

"Let's hope the sheriff agrees."

14

Morgan stood behind Avril as she locked up, his back to her. A dark thought struck. The person trying to kill her and implicate him in her and her sister's murder—if that was the case here—could be anywhere. Literally.

Using a gun as a murder weapon wouldn't make sense because the weapon would have to somehow be able to be tied back to him.

Speaking of which, he double-checked his Colt .45 was still inside his gym bag before tucking it behind the driver's seat in its usual spot. It was. He thought about the other weapons in his home. He kept a shotgun on hand. That was about it. There would be holes in a prosecutor's case who couldn't prove gunpowder on his hands. Then again, an argument could be made for him wearing gloves. There were ways around every defense. He issued a sharp sigh.

What about the phone call? He'd been the second person she'd called after being run off the road. Morgan didn't own an oversized truck or any kind of vehicle with bigger than normal tires. The family at the scene could testify to as much. They'd been there by the time Morgan arrived. Couldn't cell towers prove he'd been home? Of course, there weren't many cell towers in Lone Star Pass, so that might not make a hill of beans difference.

Was there enough circumstantial evidence mounting to accuse him of a heinous crime? To arrest him? To put him through a trial? To threaten his freedom?

What happened to Spicy Peanut might have been a message. The bastard could hit where it hurt. He could access the ranch and get inside the barn whenever he wanted to. Would this cause the law to look to his family for suspects? Or to ranch hands?

Morgan's thoughts were spiraling. His mood soured. And he'd never felt more helpless in his life than the time he couldn't pull a calf out of the mud hold it sank into. The calf had drowned. He remembered the moment to this day. The frustration that had engulfed him with nowhere to go. The anger that had threatened to burn him from the inside out.

The feeling had been too familiar while growing up in the Firebrand house.

To an outsider, a case could be built out of his dysfunctional family dynamic. They could say he harbored resentment toward women because of his mother. They could pick apart a family that was finally trying to heal. And they would be correct on many aspects. Enough truth to plant seeds in a jury's mind that would make them believe he was capable of committing such an act against a woman.

But how would they explain Spicy Peanut?

To be fair, thirty years was a good life span for a horse. Ponies usually lived longer.

Morgan gripped the steering wheel tighter. So many

good childhood memories involved the animals, and Spicy Peanut was certainly a big part of them.

A glance over at Avril said her mind was spinning out too. She'd just learned a search party was on the hunt for her sister, a recovery mission more so than a rescue.

Her face muscles were tense, and she chewed on her fingernail as she stared out the front window, clearly lost in thought.

"This bastard won't get away," was all he could manage to say. At this point, Mazie might actually be gone. The fact that she'd been too quiet and her cell phone had had no recent activity weren't good signs. Plus, if this was a revenge situation, the bastard was calculating, biding his time until all the right pieces fell in place.

Dammit.

Morgan didn't want to get ahead of himself, because sometimes hope was the only thing holding someone together. He didn't want to believe Mazie was gone or that they'd find her body on his family's property.

Lawler was sending a deputy to help spearhead the hunt. Too much time had passed and it made no sense the bastard would keep Mazie alive. There was only one shred of hope to hold onto, and that was the fact a body hadn't been discovered yet.

"Who could do such a thing?" Avril asked quietly.

"The question might be who could hate my family so much they'd want revenge," he said. "Then again, this would be more than revenge. This would be persecution and torture."

"Is it wrong that I'm still holding out hope that my sister is still alive?" Avril asked, her voice small. Vulnerable.

"I don't intend to give up hope until proven otherwise," he said. "Until then, there's always a reason to hold onto the positive. Sometimes, it's all we have to keep us stitched together."

She nodded.

"For what it's worth, everyone back home is hoping this turns out well," he said. "They'll pull together and find her if she's there."

"I just hope we aren't searching for her body," Avril said after stifling a sniffle.

"Either way, I'm right here," he reassured.

She chewed the nail until he thought it might bleed. "Unless the twisted judicial system locks away an innocent man."

It meant a lot to him that she didn't question his innocence.

"It happens," she continued. "It's unbelievable but it does happen."

"I know," he said, thinking he would spend every last dime he had to prove his innocence if that was what it took. Even thinking about the possibility of needing a lawyer hit hard.

But then, life was a twisty, turning, ever-changing proposition full of potholes and diversions. The minute he thought he might have it figured out, life changed course and proved him wrong.

It was easy to get lulled into thinking every day would be the same or guaranteed. His mother's actions and subsequent arrest reminded him of the unpredictable nature of things. He would never take another simple day for granted.

Because not being out on the land he loved, being able to work cattle and breathe the air, made him feel out of place. Nature made sense to him. There were predators and prey. Animals didn't kill for the thrill of it. They only killed what they could eat. Nature took care of the body too, causing it to degrade and replenish the earth after everything useful had been taken from it.

There was something reassuring about the seasons despite the unpredictable weather within them. Still, every August, the heat would threaten to buckle roads and melt flip-flops as they walked across hot concrete. Winters would be a mix of sunny days, cold days, and sleet. None of it would stick around long. The old saying proved true every time, *if you don't like Texas weather, stick around five minutes because it'll change.*

"We're heading to the main house, by the way," he said as he turned off the farm road and toward the security booth.

"What the...?" she asked but stopped herself from finishing.

A gate opened, so he drove through. "This was my grandfather's house."

The two-story brick house had been described by most as one of the grandest personal homes they'd ever seen.

"This yard looks like a golf course," she said as she looked around, taking it all in. "It's easy to forget your family practically prints money, considering you're one of the most down-to-earth people I've ever met."

"Thank you, I think," he said, pretty sure it was a compliment.

"I didn't mean that in the way it came out," she said. "I'm just saying that most people would come out different, if they grew up in a place like this."

"Then, you haven't met many ranchers," he pointed out. "We grow up working the land and taking care of animals. I'd like to say we take care of each other, but in my family that's more of a recent change. Usually, though, ranchers take care of others like they take care of their own. It's ingrained in us from a young age."

"Still," she said.

"Money is important, don't get me wrong, but my mother is a prime example of it never being enough," he said. "Her greed is what landed her behind bars. And she had all this too."

"Some people are never happy, no matter how good they have it," she reasoned. "My father had a wonderful wife and two girls who wanted to love him. But he chose a life of crime."

"Addiction can be an awful thing," he agreed.

"Why two identical barns?" she asked as he passed by the house where his grandfather had lived while he was alive.

"Because my grandfather believed winning was everything, so he pitted my father and uncle against each other their entire lives," he said. "Which also proves not everyone is cut out for parenting."

"What about your grandmother?"

He didn't have time to answer the question as he pulled in between the barn and a deputy's SUV. A small crowd was gathered around the deputy.

Morgan parked. "Are you ready to meet the family?"

~

AVRIL TOOK IN A SHARP BREATH. "Ready as I'll ever be."

"I'll introduce you to them personally once we find your sister alive," Morgan said with conviction.

She offered a smile before exiting the truck and joining the group of six.

The deputy acknowledged their presence with a nod but

kept talking. "You two take this area." He pointed to a spot on a hand-drawn map.

All six men standing in a semi-circle looked related. They were all tall, ranging in height from six-feet-two-inches to six-feet-four-inches, and had similar builds. To her thinking, Morgan was the best looking of the bunch but they would all be considered attractive by most standards. She wouldn't argue. Tall and handsome seemed to be the Firebrand family gene pool.

"Okay," one of the guys said before walking over and pulling Morgan into a bear hug. Two by two, they took their assignments gave a quick hug and a nod toward Avril before heading out.

There was something about the way they were pulling together that tugged at Avril's heart. The picture of big family Christmases around a table full of food and laughter hit her.

A rogue tear welled and then ran down her cheek. Morgan noticed because he squeezed her hand in the way he always did when he was trying to offer comfort and reassurance. She wanted family holidays for her and she wanted them for Mazie. They'd only had each other once their mother died. Not that Avril could complain. She'd had the most time with their mother, having been the oldest by quite a large spread. Was it too late?

"Where do you want us, Deputy?" Morgan asked.

"Why don't you cover this area," he said, pointing to an area left of where they currently stood.

"My home is this way," Morgan pointed out, gesturing the opposite direction.

"I know," the deputy said. "I'm Larse, by the way."

Morgan's jaw muscle clenched. After a quick round of introductions, Larse got on his radio.

"Why doesn't he want us near your house?" she asked Morgan when the deputy was distracted.

"I don't know for certain, but if I had to guess, I'd say he doesn't want us to be the ones to find her if she's here," he supplied, still visibly tense.

"Because?"

"Other than the fact it would be traumatizing for you, it might look bad for the investigation if I'm the one who finds her," he said with a look of apology.

"Oh," she said, realizing the law might be on Morgan's side and trying to protect him. The gesture was good but it served to remind them both he was still a suspect, and this situation didn't look good for him.

"Plus, they need this other area scanned anyway in order to cover all the bases on the property," Morgan explained. "And then there is the very real possibility the bastard is out here."

"Why would he do that?" she asked. "Why would he stick around with all this heat?"

"He knew that you were visiting me," he supplied.

Avril muttered a curse. "I didn't even think about the fact he might have been still watching your home."

"If this is connected to my family, it makes sense he is keeping an eye on me," Morgan pointed out. "Setting me up for charges that could put me away for life would be one way to get back at my mother. Funny thing about it is that she doesn't care about anyone but herself."

"I'm sure she cares in her own way," she said, hoping she wasn't stepping on his toes with the comment. "Even though from everything you've said, she sounds like a self-centered person."

"Not enough to get her act together," he said under his breath.

Avril wished there was some way she could take away his pain. She was all too familiar with the sting of rejection, especially when it came to a parent who was supposed to offer love and protection.

She reached out for his hand and gave a gentle squeeze of reassurance. "Every child should feel loved by both parents. It should be a birthright."

"Agreed," he said with disdain in his tone. "Which is exactly the reason I never plan to have children of my own."

"Same," she concurred.

"You?" he said, but it was more statement than question. "You'll make an amazing mother some day, when you're ready."

"I won't, and I'll never be ready," she argued.

"Your choice as to whether or not you'll want them, but I'll push back on the fact you'd be an amazing mother," he said with the kind of certainty that almost had her believing it too.

She cocked her head to the side, curious. "Why?"

"Because you don't give up when you love someone," he said. "Look at the lengths you're going to find your sister. You are loyal almost to a fault. I have a feeling if you could ever let yourself love someone, you'd love big. And you know what it's like to be abandoned, so you would never allow that to happen to a child of yours. A kid would be lucky to have you for a mother."

Why did those statements cause an ache deep in her chest? A longing for a life she had never known, let alone wanted?

"I might not ever consider walking out on a child of mine, but I can't control someone else's actions," she said. "I have no other family and my sister, when we find her, certainly wouldn't be able to take care of someone else. She can barely handle her own life. If anything happened to me, and the dad decided not to stick around, where would that leave a kid?"

"Life throws a helluva lot of curve balls," he agreed. "No one knows what's going to happen today, let alone tomorrow. And yet, I feel confident in saying you would never allow your child to suffer the same fate as you and your sister. Not if there was a breath left in your body."

He had that right. And the best way to make certain of the fact was to close that door altogether. Although, she had to admit being with someone like Morgan could change her mind. He embodied all the qualities he'd just described. If they were together, she could almost see having a family as possible. Almost.

Morgan's cell buzzed. He checked the screen. And then he released a string of curse words.

"They found her."

Those three words buckled Avril's knees.

15

"She's alive," Morgan was relieved to be able to say as he caught Avril before she stumbled and fell.

"I have to go to her," Avril said, turning back the second she got her sea legs.

He shook his head. "Larse is asking you to go home."

"What?" she asked, incredulous. "There's no way I'm—"

"Before you protest too much, more messages are coming through," he interrupted. "It looks like the grave was fresh and your sister is critical. Help is on the way and she is receiving life-saving measures on the scene." He paused as he caught up reading texts. "The perp is possibly still in the area. Larse is changing his tune, asking you to go somewhere safe on property now, not home. The sheriff is on his way to the ranch. They want the whole area on lockdown while they comb through the property."

"What am I supposed to do with this, Morgan?" she asked, biting down on her bottom lip. She shook her head. "I need to see her with my own eyes. I need to see that she's going to be okay. What if my presence could mean the difference between her pulling through or not? I have to go to the hospital."

"The sheriff says no," he continued. "They are worried he might find you on the road like before and then you wouldn't be any good to your sister."

"It'll draw him out," she said, continuing down a desperate trail. "They can't argue with me there. It might be the only way to catch the bastard."

"You want to be used as bait?" he asked, before shaking his head. "Hell no. I'd rather go by myself and find another way to lure him out."

She opened her mouth to protest, but he stopped her by gently wrapping his hands around her wrists.

"They found her," he said. "She's alive. She'll be protected from here on out. Now, we need to focus on becoming invisible. It's the best way to protect her and you." He would beg if he had to. "I have no shame here. I'm asking you to stick with me so I can find a place to keep you safe until the sheriff locates the bastard who did this to your family and mine. Your sister might be able to give clues as to who is responsible now that she's been found."

He didn't add the part about her needing to live. It wouldn't do any good or help improve the odds Avril would listen to him.

Based on the fact she was biting hard on her bottom lip, he was making progress. He also needed to force his gaze away from those pink lips of hers because this wasn't the time for desire to well up inside him like a rogue wave. The need to kiss her was a physical ache. She touched a place deep inside that had been closed off up until now. She was the only one who'd ever gotten close, let alone break through those walls. He'd locked that part of himself off years ago and threw away the key, never to darken that door again. Or so he'd believed.

Now that she'd awakened the need in him, it was going to be impossible to walk away from her until he knew she was safe. No one had brought out all his protective instincts in the way Avril did. To be fair, she was capable of taking care of herself, but the simple act of making food for her gave him a whole new-to-him level of satisfaction.

"What do you think?" he asked as she stood there. She'd pulled her wrists back and then folded her arms across her chest. Half a dozen emotions played out across her features, most notably anger and helplessness.

He knew those feelings all too well lately.

"This guy isn't going to be easy to find," she conceded on a sharp exhale.

"Which is why we wait," he said. He could guess how she was feeling because he would be going through the same emotions. The bastard was close, and it seemed like a waste to let him get away. But trying to use her as bait didn't guarantee the perp would show up or that anyone could save Avril if he did. "He might suspect you'll make a public display to draw him out. He could be one step ahead."

"We won't know if we don't try," she argued, but there wasn't a whole lot of conviction in her tone.

"That's true," he said. "But I can't lose you. Not on my watch."

An emotion passed behind her eyes that he couldn't quite pinpoint. He hoped it meant she understood how deeply he cared.

Avril issued a sharp sigh. "I know you're right. I do. But this is the hardest thing I've ever been through."

"I'm right here," he said in as calm a voice as he could muster. "You don't have to go through any of this alone."

Her arms folded across her chest were the equivalent of a barricade. A wall had come up between them and her body language made it clear. She stared at him with a look that almost dared him to speak. Her lips thinned. Her pupils dilated. Her stare intensified.

"I'm here," he repeated. "You don't have to go through it alone."

"You really shouldn't..."

Her words started off fiery but then calmed down as she let the thought trail off.

"I'm here," he repeated for the third time. "You don't have to go through it alone."

"Morgan," she managed to get out as a few tears escaped and dripped down her cheeks.

So, he took a step toward her, closing more of the space between them. She brought her gaze up to meet his as he thumbed away her tears.

"This shouldn't be happening to you or Mazie," he said, hearing the gruff quality to his own voice. "I'm sorry."

"You didn't do this to us," she said, dropping her gaze to his shirt but leaning toward him. Her arms were still folded across her chest, but her shoulders relaxed with an exhale.

"Not personally, no," he said. "But evidence is pointing heavily to this being my family's fault. Someone is coming after me. And all I can think about is making sure you come out of this alive. I can't let anything happen to you. My conscience wouldn't survive."

"That the only reason?" she asked, not making eye contact. "Because you feel responsible for what is happening to me and my sister."

Could he let himself go there with her? Talk about how he truly felt? Did he even know what she meant to him? Because he took this seriously and he needed to get his emotions in check. Morgan wasn't the type of person to get caught up in the moment, so this threw him for a loop.

"I'm not going to disagree with you there," he stated. "I do feel responsible. I also realize I didn't ask for any of this and neither did you. But, hear me out."

She nodded.

"There's someone out there who is setting me up for murder," he continued. "I don't know who it is or why. I can only guess this is related to my mother's actions, but I could have angered someone in the past. It could be a poacher that I personally hunted down. There's no telling until we catch the bastard. Using you as bait isn't an option for me. I'd tell you to go far away from me to stay as safe as possible, except that I think this animal will come for you anyway."

Avril stood there but dropped her hands to her sides.

"So, that makes me responsible," he said. "And I can't stand the thought of anything happening to you. I wouldn't survive it."

Her gaze locked onto his.

"Please, let me take you somewhere to hide out," he said. "I might know a good place to go while the sheriff, deputies, and rest of the family track this sonofabitch down."

"What makes you think they will be successful?"

"I have to believe they will," he said. "They found Mazie. If she's able to speak, she might be able to give them a name."

"I need to see her," she said, exhaling out some of the frustration. "But I won't do anything that puts her in greater danger." She twisted her fingers together. "Okay. Where do you want to go?"

∽

AVRIL PULLED on every ounce of willpower she had not to run to the site or the hospital to see Mazie. She had no idea what condition her sister was in, but it couldn't be good if the sheriff didn't want Avril anywhere near her sister.

Morgan's cell buzzed. "The sheriff has a first name. Does Decker ring any bells?"

"No," she said, shaking her head. "Not for me. What about you?"

"We had a ranch hand years ago who we used to call Deck, but I can't recall if that's from his last name or not," he supplied. "Normally, nicknames come from the last name."

"It's a start," she said, hope trying to seed in her heart.

"This is good progress," he said. "The sheriff also said Mazie is in an ambulance on the way to the hospital."

"Did he say anything about her condition?" she asked, perking up a little more with the news.

"No, he didn't," Morgan said as he sent a response.

They had a name. It was something to work with. "Did you tell him about Deck?"

"I did just now," Morgan acknowledged.

It was taking everything inside Avril not to lean into his strength. It wouldn't take much to unravel her at this point despite the nuggets of good news. "What did he say?"

Morgan read the screen. "That my brothers and cousins already supplied the information."

Staying out of the way under normal circumstances would make sense. In this case, it would be the most difficult thing she'd ever done. Could she let go of the lonely feeling that had plagued her for her entire life? Funny how habits kept her thinking the same patterns despite mounting evidence to the contrary. Morgan was here. His family was here. And it was a very large family at that.

"They have everything under control for now," Morgan

said, lifting his gaze to make eye contact. "Are you ready to go?"

She paused for a few moments, taking her time. Once she agreed, there would be no turning back. And yet, she knew leaving was the most logical choice.

"Okay," she said. "How far is it to your place?"

"We're not going there," he said. "We have no idea if Decker is watching my home or acting alone."

"Or if Decker is even the person's real name," she said. She would believe it if she heard it from Mazie's mouth, but since there was no context, she didn't want to fall into a trap that might lead her down the wrong direction.

As it was, she searched her brain for anyone with a first or last name of Decker. Came up empty. And then it dawned on her. "We can check the comments section on my sister's channel. Maybe find someone there."

"I'm sure the sheriff is already on it, but it's a good idea," he said. "We'll have good WiFi at the barn."

"A barn?"

"It's where I'm taking you," he said, reaching for her hand. A calmness like she'd never known came over her body and soul with the connection. By this point, she was used to the spark that also came with contact and it gave a sense of familiarity that she'd grown accustomed to. "It belongs to the other side of the family. It's where Raleigh Perry wrote the number one song on the country charts."

"Is your cousin really married to her?" Avril asked.

"Brax?" Morgan asked, but it was more statement than question. "That's a fact."

"That's actually cool," she said, using anything as a distraction. If she kept her mind thinking about how badly she missed her sister, there was no way she wasn't driving straight to the hospital. Another thought struck. "What about a law enforcement escort to the hospital? Wouldn't that solve a lot of problems?" Clearly, she wasn't quite ready to let this topic go.

"It would be nice if it was that easy," he said. "But, no, I think it complicates matters because the sheriff isn't going to want to take resources away from the investigation. He might have several leads at this point."

Was it too good to be true? Was this nightmare close to being over?

As much as Avril wanted her life to go back to normal, she couldn't help but wonder what normal was anymore. Because normal felt like being with Morgan. And that was misguided at best and a recipe for heartbreak at worst. Losing him wouldn't be like other breakups. He would shatter her world, leaving her heart in a thousand tiny flecks to be swept up. He had a life here in Lone Star Pass. He had family here and loved his work. She had a business to run. Her home was on the outskirts of Austin, where she enjoyed pizza delivery and, hell, all kinds of food delivery. She couldn't live without her conveniences. Could she?

Although, being here on the ranch with Morgan had brought a sense of calm over her like she'd never known before. Even in the midst of her life spiraling out of control with her sister, Morgan was her center.

A noise to her left stopped her in her tracks. Morgan stopped too. He also brought a protective hand up to tuck her behind him. Given his size and heft, she didn't mind. Besides, she could be lethal from behind him as much as out front. This would give her a few extra seconds to react, which could mean the difference between life and death if the other person wasn't expecting her to fight.

She glanced around the ground for anything she could

use as a weapon, dropping down to palm a jagged-edged rock. It fit nicely in her hand and would do some damage.

Twigs breaking underneath footsteps had Morgan inching the two of them behind a tree. He reached around and pulled a Colt .45 out of the waistband of his jeans. He held up a hand, putting his index finger to his lips.

Avril had no problems being quiet, listening. She was ready to attack, praying this could be the Decker person her sister had mentioned.

Even so, her pulse pounded and her erratic heartbeat made her slow her breathing to calm down. That was the thing about self-defense, no one truly knew how their body would adapt to the surge of adrenaline that came with fear. Practice helped develop muscle memory. It would help her adjust to the boost that could create superpowers.

Her hand trembled and she could feel her heart pounding the inside of her ribcage. As far as flight or freeze instincts went, most people left out the fight response because it was rare. She threw a fist before asking questions. Mazie had always had a freeze instinct. It was another in a long list of reasons Avril had always felt protective of her baby sister.

Mazie was alive. Avril let those words seed after fearing her sister would never be found. Or worse, would be found too late.

The thought of seeing her sister again, of hugging her, gave Avril a renewed resolve to find the bastard responsible and fight if this was him. And, yes, she could let the sheriff do his job too.

Morgan held up two fingers. Yep, she'd heard two distinct sets of boots.

And they were coming closer.

16

Morgan was still searching the back of his mind to find any reference to Decker, Deck, or Decks other than the ranch hand from years ago. Deck had worked at Firebrand at least six years ago. He'd barely been seventeen and strong as an ox back then. Decker Gambit. What would he have against Morgan, especially after all this time? Or was Morgan first in a long line of revenge plans?

Avril's body was flush against his back. He could feel her rapid heartbeat against him. Her breathing was measured, no doubt one of the self-defense tricks to keep from full-scale panicking.

Another twig snapped not twenty feet away from them. The breeze carried the low hum of a pair of male voices in their direction.

Right now, the best thing they could do was keep a low profile. Whoever was out there, and he guessed it was a pair of his brothers or cousins, would be better off not knowing their location. He highly doubted the footsteps belonged to the person responsible for bringing Mazie here. It seemed one person was responsible, which made sense.

Once they got to the barn, he could check his cell phone to see if anyone calling themselves Deck had commented on Avril's post. He'd take any direction they could get. Having law enforcement work on the case would double the progress at the very least. And then there was his family to consider, who were in the mix. They were relentless and had plenty of experience tracking poachers. Granted, people who stalked animals were different kinds of humans than folks who went after people. But there had to be enough similarity to increase the odds of catching up to the bastard if he was still on the property.

The footsteps disappeared after another couple of minutes. Morgan deemed it safe enough to travel. The trick was going to be getting into the barn without being recognized. His cousins' barn had a loft where the two of them should be safe once they reached their destination.

It wouldn't be dark for hours and they needed food if they were going to make it through the day, let alone night. There were offices in the barn and a restroom. It occurred to him that his truck was parked near the barns by the main house. That was another problem. Of course, his emergency supplies that he kept in his gym bag would be enough to keep them going for the night. Did he dare hope the perp would be caught by then?

Law enforcement had to be getting close. Right? Now that Mazie had been found and had given them a name, the sheriff should be able to work quickly. He wouldn't share the details of what he had while an investigation was in full force, so Morgan figured Lawler knew more than he could or would say.

The sheriff would, however, call or text when the perp

was in handcuffs. Morgan didn't have to reach out to ask Lawler to keep them posted. He trusted the man knew they'd be hanging on the edge of their seats until word came down.

But what should he do about his truck? He could text to have one of his family members take it home and leave it. Actually, he liked the idea. He pulled out his cell and then checked for service.

None.

Not surprising, there were more dead spots than not on the ranch. He'd send the message as soon as he got bars. This probably wasn't the time to regret not carrying a satellite phone with him.

"Is it a good idea for us to show up at the barn in broad daylight?" Avril asked.

"Probably not," he said.

"Think we should camp out here for the rest of the day before heading back?" she continued.

"I know you don't like it out here," he said, hearing the slight tremble in her voice.

"Not, but I'd rather be safe than sorry," she admitted. Her reasoning was sound but the last thing he needed was to be out here after dark when it would be impossible to see a foot in front of them. As much as he knew this property and was comfortable, the same couldn't be said for Avril. She was mentally strong but everyone had a breaking point.

"What about food?" he asked. "You have to be getting hungry by now."

"I can wait," she said, walking right behind him. "Is there water? I could use a drink."

"There's a stream not too far from here," he replied. She was holding up well but for how much longer? Knowing her sister was in the hospital without being briefed on her condition must be eating her from the inside out. "As soon as I get service, I can check with one of my relatives to get the low-down about Mazie's condition."

"I'd appreciate it," she said. "Any chance they'd be willing to keep watch over her at the hospital? I know she's being looked after and yet I have a sinking feeling she needs more."

"Do you think the perp would show up there to finish the job?"

"Anything's possible at this point," she said. "If the bastard is watching, he might know she's been found."

"It would stand to reason she'd be taken to the ER," he said. "Do you know if my profile picked her or if she picked me?"

She shook her head. "I don't..." She snapped her fingers. "Actually, I remember cautioning her about meeting people from one of those sites. She told me not to worry because it's the kind where the woman picks first."

Anyone could have been this jerk's victim. It just happened to be Mazie. He wouldn't wish that on anyone, but he could honestly say that he was grateful to have met Avril. He only wished they'd met under better circumstances.

"I'm sorry it was her," he said.

"She's alive," Avril said quietly. "That's the only thing that matters other than putting this bastard behind bars and throwing away the key."

"Agreed." The wall she'd put up from earlier was back. Could he break through it again? Stay on the other side?

Morgan led her to the stream he'd spent a good portion of his childhood splashing around in. The water wouldn't be drinkable but, if memory served and no one had come around here, there should be an iron kettle tucked inside a tree hollow. Since it was still daylight, he could make a small fire without drawing attention to their location. Exactly the reason he carried flint in his pocket along with a small knife. It was habit after spending too many years waking up and heading out before the sun was up, not returning until after dark while working cattle.

What folks didn't realize was most of working cattle dealt with running fences, making repairs as needed to ensure the safety of the herd. The other part of the job had to do with paperwork, and the other side of the family swam in it most times. He didn't mind not having to enter every detail about the health of the herd, not to mention each individual calf's specific details into the computer. While most ranchers used trucks for herding, Firebrand was rooted in tradition. They rode horseback and ATVs for fence work. There was something humbling about taking out his mare rain or shine that made him feel more connected to ranching life.

It took a second to find the exact location of the kettle, but it was still there. He ran it through the water as Avril gathered rocks. She made a small circle and then found enough sticks to start a decent fire.

He stopped and stared at her for a long moment before she looked up. "Do I want to ask how you know what I plan to do, given the fact you don't like the outdoors much?"

She cracked a small smile. "Did you ever ask why I don't like 'em?"

He shook his head.

"When it was the three of us, my dad—if you can call him that—used to force us to go camping because he'd decided there would be an apocalypse or alien invasion. We were going to survive." She shook her head. "So, we had these drills we had to do because he was convinced we were going to need to know this. Problem was he would bring a bottle of liquor, drink most of it, and then pass out in the woods. We'd have to go looking for him in the middle of the night, because he would take the truck keys with him. He was especially fond of taking us out during spring thunderstorms or when the weatherman predicted cold."

Morgan's hands fisted at the thought she'd been forced to endure this as a child. He thought he knew all about the kind of bad parenting that leaves scars for the rest of one's life, but this was right up there. He was also beginning to understand how deep her need to protect herself ran. And how unlikely it was that she would keep her guard down for long with anyone, including him.

∼

"I JUST OVERSHARED," Avril said, unable to hide her embarrassment. "I never talk about stuff like that with anyone, not even my sister."

"Does she know what you were put through?" he asked.

"No," Avril stated. "The past is the past, right? It's not like we can change it by continuing to bring it up. Otherwise, I'd be the first to shout it from the rooftops or tell everyone within five minutes of meeting them."

Morgan didn't immediately speak. "I've never been one to rehash the past, either. But I'm starting to believe getting it out in the open isn't such a bad thing. Not because we want pity but because it's part of our story. It's part of what makes us who we are and why we make the decisions we do. It's part of us that can't be denied."

He punctuated his thoughts by taking a knee next to the teepee made of sticks she'd set up, struck the sharp edge of the flint against a small blade, and then sat back on his heel when the spark started a small fire.

On top of the teepee, he placed a kettle half filled with water.

"How did you know that was going to be out here?" she asked, motioning toward the kettle.

"I didn't for sure," he responded with a small smile that stirred her heart. As much as she wanted—no needed—to keep her defenses up with this man, it was proving harder than she wanted it to be.

She knew a thing or two about guilt. It was there in his eyes and on his face. He would always blame himself for what happened to her and her sister. If Mazie didn't make it through this...

Avril couldn't go there, not even hypothetically. Her sister had to survive. The two of them had been through way too much together for it to end now, like this.

"Nick and I spent a lot of time out here when we were kids," he explained. "Hell, the whole lot of us bounced in and out between the eighteen of us. We played sports, did our work, and pretty much stayed out of sight of the adults as much as possible. We strategically placed supplies around, using tree hollows in the place of cabinets. That way, we wouldn't have to go back for water."

"I can't even imagine growing up in such a big family," she said, bewildered. They had time to kill, and she wanted to know more about what it was like to grow up as a Firebrand on a ranch. "You said there were nine boys on each side. How many sets of twins?"

"One," he supplied. "Believe it or not. And then my cousin Brax is technically our half cousin, but my aunt took him in as though he was her own and none of us knew any different until recently."

"That must have come as a shock," she said.

"I still feel for Brax, but he has made peace with it and none of us will ever look at him as anything other than one hundred percent our cousin or brother," he supplied.

"I always envisioned having a big family," she said in another show of honesty that caught her off guard. "You know what I mean, like the picture-perfect version. It was just me for so long and the age difference between Mazie and I was too big for us to be going through the same things at the same time. What was it like to have so many brothers and cousins?"

"Someone was always in a big blowout fight, and someone always had my back," he said with a laugh. "It was chaos because the family was too divided, thanks to our grandfather."

"Still," she said. "Having eight brothers must have been interesting."

"Not one homemade ham at Christmas if that's what you're thinking," he quickly added. "There were no cookies baking in the oven in our house. That all happened across the way at my aunt's place. We've had more than our fair share of drama. My brother Kellan married Liv, who is now married to my cousin Corbin."

"Do I even want to know the story behind that?" she asked with a laugh.

"It's a mess," he said. "But I think the two have since buried the hatchet. Liv and Corbin were best friends growing up and everyone could see how much they loved each other. Everyone but the two of them, that is. Corbin ended up getting engaged to someone else, so Kellan seized the opportunity and swooped in. Liv lost her mother and was vulnerable. I think she needed someone to lean on, and Kellan jumped at the chance. To be fair, his feelings for her were real. My older brother is stubborn, so his new wife leaving him didn't go over well. He may say everything is okay, but I imagine he's still licking wounds over that situation."

"Who wouldn't be?" she asked, realizing size didn't matter when it came to family drama. In fact, it could be multiplied in larger families. "At least you guys have each other to lean on when life throws a fastball at your face."

"That much is true," he conceded. "And I wouldn't trade being from a big family for the world. It might not be all sunshine and roses, but there's always someone around to have your back. Now that our grandfather is gone and can't create more infighting, we're starting to heal and behave like people who actually care about each other."

"Getting older helps with that, don't you think?" she asked. "In my twenties, I didn't think I needed anyone. I'm ashamed to say that I looked at my sister as a burden more times than not."

"We start off in this life the most selfish we'll ever be," he reasoned. "If you don't believe me, spend the day around a two-year-old." He laughed, and it was as though someone peeled back the tree branches overhead and let the sun shine through.

"Oh, I avoid those little critters like the plague," she teased back, grateful for a reprieve from the heaviness of the day so far. It would be short-lived. She had no idea what was happening with her sister, so she held onto the thread of information that was fact. Her sister was alive and getting the absolute best possible care.

"And then we start realizing at some point there's a whole other world besides the one we live in inside our own heads," he said. "We learn not to hurt other people's feelings after our mind is blown that other people actually have them." He laughed, and it was the best sound she'd heard. "Teenage years seem to revert us back but it's only temporary because our twenties are not far behind, and that's when we grow into who we're meant to be."

"At thirty-three, you would have thought I'd have it all figured out," she quipped. But then, she never really opened herself up to anyone before in the way she did with Morgan.

A bubbling noise came from the kettle. Morgan grabbed a stick and removed it from the fire before dousing out the small flames.

"Don't tell me you have cups over there somewhere," Avril said, surprised when he then produced a pair of tin coffee cups.

"We were resourceful," he said on another laugh. "What can I say?"

"Are these gems hidden all over the property?" she asked, thinking it would make it easier for a stalker to camp out. Probably poachers too.

"Most of the real danger happens out there," he said motioning deeper into the thicket. "No one comes this close to the houses unless they want to get caught," he said. "As you saw when we arrived, there's security on patrol and in the box at the gate to control which vehicles come onto the land. My home isn't as secure because I'm far from the main house, which is just the way I wanted it."

"You're breaking down all my preconceived notions about big families and rich people," she said. "It actually sounds kind of awful to have to protect your home with paid security. Always be on guard."

"When you're a Firebrand, you also have a whole bunch of expectations on you from pretty much everyone in town," he added. "And anyone who knows your name within the state."

"I pretty much slipped through life unnoticed," she said, not realizing what a blessing that probably had been.

"I highly doubt that," he said. "You're far too beautiful to go unnoticed."

Avril felt a red blush crawl up her neck. Rather than let herself get too lost in the moment or ask for another kiss, she decided her water needed cooling. It was too hot to drink, and her mouth had suddenly gone dry again. She moved over to the water and put the base of her tin cup in the cool stream. Morgan did the same. As much as she'd hated all those drills in her childhood, she liked being able to hold her own outdoors.

It didn't take long to cool off the water inside the tin. She drank it down in a matter of seconds. She'd also learned that staying in one place too long was never a good idea.

Another twig snapping caused every muscle in her body to tense. Someone was out there. Someone quiet. Did that someone spot her?

17

Morgan crouched down low and then army-crawled out of sight, urging Avril to follow. A glance back said she'd split off.

It was probably smarter to do it this way, but he didn't like it one bit. Her being out of sight caused his stress levels to skyrocket. This seemed like a good time to remind himself that she had a base knowledge of survival. Actually, her self-defense instincts were about as solid as they come.

They'd almost made it to nightfall, so he hoped this person or persons kept on walking without stopping or talking to them. It was probably someone from the search team and nothing to worry about.

As long as they both kept a low profile, they should be okay.

"Ouch," came the male voice. Morgan recognized it despite the years in between. Decker Gambit, the ranch hand. What the hell? His voice was deeper now but this had to be him.

He must have stepped into the area of the fire. He let out

a string of curse words that would make a grandmother want to wash his mouth out with soap.

"What has that bitch done now?" Deck's voice was almost at a hysterical pitch.

"Are you talking about my sister?" Avril asked, her voice cutting through the air and alerting Deck not only to their presence but her location.

Now it was Morgan's turn to cuss. He'd planned to follow Deck until the time to strike presented itself, preferably without Avril.

When he really thought about it, there was no way she was going to let him track Deck alone.

"Neither of you will die," Deck said with a grunt as he whirled around to where Avril had stepped out from behind a tree. "Why won't either of you bitches die?"

Morgan still had the element of surprise on his side. He moved with stealth as he got a better visual of Avril standing off with Deck. The glint of metal said Deck had a weapon pointed toward Avril, most likely a gun.

Morgan bit back a curse. This was about to get even trickier. The Colt .45 Ruger Blackhawk was the most accurate revolver but even it couldn't hit a mark through a tree trunk.

Before anyone could move, the crack of a bullet split the air. Avril immediately dove behind a tree. Deck seized the opportunity to turn tail and run.

Morgan had no choice but to reveal himself. By the time he snapped to his feet, Avril was crouched down low. He couldn't get a good visual on her body to see if she'd been hit.

"I let my emotions get out of control," she said, admonishing herself. "I shouldn't have done that."

"Forget that, are you hit?" he asked, frantic.

She looked her body up and down. "No. I don't think so."

"Stay right here," he warned. "I'll be right back."

The sound of her footsteps behind him shouldn't surprise him as he bolted after Deck. The younger man was fast on his feet, and Morgan struggled to keep up, let alone try to make ground. Firing was impossible unless his goal was to take bits of bark off a tree. Hitting his mark while the man wound through the thicket would be next to impossible, even for a good shot like Morgan.

Deck had thinned out and had more of a runners build, which wasn't helping with the chase. Morgan had no doubt the young man was still strong. Underestimating Deck would be a mistake.

Could Morgan distract him?

"I know who you are. The law knows you're here. What the hell did I ever do to you, Deck?" Morgan shouted.

"That bitch of a mother of yours got a little too greedy," Deck shot back. He half turned and got off a wild shot.

The bullet went wide, and splintered part of a tree.

Morgan glanced back because it was too quiet back there. Avril was nowhere to be seen. Was she hit and didn't realize it before? Had she stumbled? Was she back there bleeding out?

Panic engulfed him but he couldn't stop now. Not when he was this close to catching the bastard. If he let Deck go, Avril would continue to be in danger. Her sister would continue to be in danger. Morgan's family would continue to be in danger.

No, this stopped here and now.

Morgan lifted his Colt .45, and then fired. He missed, but the distraction caused Deck to slam into a tree branch as he turned around to see what had just happened. Or, should Morgan say, a tree branch slammed into Deck.

Deck's gun flew out of his hand as he grabbed at a nearby tree trunk, trying to break his own fall. With a grunt, he threw himself toward the weapon that had fired a third bullet. A Glock 23 could have ten more rounds, so Morgan needed to get to the weapon before the bastard got hold of it and pulled off a real shot.

Morgan launched himself toward Deck, missed by an inch. He cursed as the younger man scrambled for the weapon that was just out of reach.

Clawing his way toward the young man, who had to be at least six feet tall, Morgan struggled for purchase as he army-crawled. As he threw an elbow up, the heel of a boot slammed into his forearm. Morgan grunted as pain shot through him. He ground his back teeth and bit back a curse.

The younger man might have been a good runner, but Morgan could out-power him if he could get hold of an ankle, foot, or calve.

"Jackie was supposed to split the money," Deck spit out before looking straight at Avril, who appeared between two trees. "We were supposed to be partners but she got greedy." He glared as Morgan used the distraction to jump onto his legs.

Deck kicked and twisted as Morgan clasped the man's thighs. The young man got off a wild punch that made Morgan see stars. He shook it off, knowing full well any slip could give an advantage to his opponent.

The next thing he knew, Avril had a branch the equivalent size of a baseball bat.

"Your bitch of a sister should have stayed buried," Deck ground out.

That was all it took for Avril to swing. The tip connected

with Deck's cheekbone. A crack sounded, which was probably bone breaking.

"That's for Mazie," Avril said, winding up to fire off another swing.

Morgan wrestled for control of Deck's arms as Avril connected the tip of the makeshift bat a second time. Blood squirted from Deck's nose, his eyes rolled back in his head, and he passed out.

"I've got it from here," Morgan said to her, unsure of how long Deck would be out. The guy would wake up fighting, though. Morgan was certain of it. "Take my phone and call the sheriff. Find cell service. It should be just over there, in the meadow. Tell him to ask Nick where it is. He'll know. Tell him about the kettle we used."

Avril took the offering and ran, disappearing into the thicket.

It felt like an eternity had passed before she returned. Darkness was setting in, but he still caught sight of the red dot flowering on her hip.

"You *were* shot," he said to her as she collapsed in front of him. The cell tumbled onto the ground as her head hit the hard dirt.

Morgan slapped Deck's face a couple of times. There was no response. The guy was out cold, which should buy some time. A few minutes? Maybe more?

After a quick scan, he figured he had at least a few minutes before Deck might stir or need to be dealt with again. He could only hope the guy wasn't waking up anytime soon because Avril was in trouble.

He abandoned sitting on Deck to attend to her as his chest squeezed. He rolled Avril onto her back, ripped off a strip of cotton from his shirt, and then pressed it into the bloody spot to stem the bleeding.

She had to be okay. There was no other option.

Morgan repeated the mantra as he maintained pressure on the wound.

Keeping one eye on Deck, Morgan held onto Avril, maintaining pressure on the wound. "Stay with me. Please. Wake up and stay with me."

It took what felt like an eternity for help to arrive, and then within minutes, the scene was flooded with first responders, siblings, and cousins.

Still, she was unconscious. Morgan was worried. He couldn't lose Avril. Not now. Not after he finally found the person he wanted to spend the rest of his life with. Not without having the chance to tell her how he felt, consequences be damned.

His chest squeezed to the point he could barely breathe as she was carried out of the thicket to the waiting stretcher in the clearing.

How would he survive if she didn't?

~

"Welcome back."

Avril blinked her eyes open and sat upright.

"Hey," Morgan's voice sent a wave of calm through her. "You're okay." His reassurance calmed her nerves a notch below panic.

"What am I doing here?" She looked around the room to get her bearings, saw that she was in the hospital. "Where's Mazie?"

Seeing Morgan first thing brought a calm over her like she'd never known.

"I thought you might have questions about your sister when you first came out of surgery," he said.

"Surgery?" she asked as he stood up and then tugged the curtain to open it.

The answer to her question had to wait because there was Mazie in the bed next to Avril's. She tried to throw off her covers to get to her sister, but Morgan was next to her in a heartbeat.

"She's going to be fine," he reassured, his voice like silk against her skin as he helped settle her underneath the covers.

"She's asleep and you've been in and out of consciousness for six hours now," he said.

The gorgeous man with a beautiful soul was a sight for sore eyes.

"Mazie?"

"Has been through a lot but your sister is going to be fine," he reassured. "Despite how this looks with all these tubes and the medication, she's doing great. She wakes up every few hours and the first word out of her mouth is your name. She asks about you and then is back asleep before anyone can answer."

"She does?" Avril's heart filled with what felt a lot like true happiness, which shouldn't be the foreign emotion it was. It had been far too long since Avril had been at peace, happy.

"It's always her first question," he repeated.

Avril took a few seconds to digest the news. She smiled before patting a spot on the bed right next to her. "Sit down with me?"

"You got it," he said. "Curtain open or closed?"

"Open," she said. "I want to see her the minute she wakes this time."

"I think that's a good idea," he said, taking a seat on the bed. He looked like he hadn't slept in days. The day-old stubble on his chin had multiplied. And yet, it only served to make him look even more beautiful in her eyes.

"What happened to Deck?" she asked.

"The bastard is going to be locked behind bars for the rest of his life," he stated. "He won't be able to harm anyone else. Justice will be served."

She was two for two on good news so far. But what she had to say next might buck the trend.

"How long have I been here?" she asked, wanting more information about her condition but also stalling before telling him what was really on her mind.

"Not quite an entire night."

"And you've been here the whole time?" she asked. He probably stuck around because the cowboy code forced him to. But she couldn't stand the thought of him walking out that door and her never seeing him again without him knowing how she felt.

"Afraid so," he said, rubbing the scruff on his chin. He lifted an arm and sniffed his pit. "Am I stinking you out? I haven't showered."

She smiled at him before shaking her head and dropping her gaze to the blanket.

"What's wrong?" he asked, concern in his tone.

She took in a deep breath and decided he was worth being brave for. If he turned her down, at least she would know and could move on with her life. Search for the connection they had that she might never find again but hoped she could at least come close. Because he'd opened her eyes to what was possible in a relationship

Lifting her gaze, she reached for his hand. It would be easier to get through this if they were touching.

"Okay, I'm just going to go for it," she whispered.

He leaned toward her, took her hand in his, and clasped their fingers together.

"I have feelings for you, Morgan," she started as he studied her. "More than that, I have fallen in love with you. And before you say anything, I know that's probably not what you want to hear because you've been nothing but kind to me, except that I could have died out there and that got me thinking about all the chances I didn't take because I was scared. I have closed myself off to so many things and people. But to be honest, I never met anyone like you before. I've never met anyone who made me want to leap out of my comfort zone so far without a safety net just because I might have the slightest chance at being with you forever."

His face gave away nothing of how those words made him feel. Was that a good sign or bad?

Either way, saying it out loud caused the boulder on her chest to loosen.

"Anyway, I just thought you should know that on the off chance you think you'd want to give us a chance," she said, then released his fingers.

"You're not getting away that easy," he said, taking her hand back and holding on. "I thought I was going to lose you out there." He stopped and his face twisted like saying the words caused physical pain. "I'm glad you're telling me this because I've fallen hard for you. I love you, Avril. And I believe what we have can go the distance. In my thirty-five years on this earth, I've never met anyone like you. Never wanted to be with someone more than I want to be with you. Never thought my heart would break into a thousand tiny pieces if I couldn't be with you. So, when you're ready, I have every intention of asking you to go the distance. So, I guess what I'm saying is, I intend to ask you to marry me."

"What if I tell you that I'm not scared?" she asked, her

heart filling up with something that felt a lot like joy. "What if I'm ready now?"

"Then we plan a wedding," he said without hesitation. Then, he leaned in for a kiss.

His lips were so tender the kiss robbed her breath.

"Get a room," came a weak voice from the bed next to them.

Avril laughed. So did Morgan.

"Great that you love each other," Mazie quipped with her trademark sarcasm. "Now, who's going to love me?"

"I never stopped, sister," Avril said with a laugh. "Welcome back, by the way."

"Congratulations," Mazie said, her voice gaining a little steam. "I hear there's going to be a wedding."

"I'm glad you're awake because I need to ask if you'd be willing to be my maid of honor," Avril said and meant it.

"I'd be honored, sis," Mazie said. "Now, when do we get out of here."

"You both need rest," Morgan stated. He turned his full attention to Avril. "I promise to love you until the day I die. And even then, I'll love you in eternity."

Avril smiled. She'd finally found someone who made her feel safe inside. And she planned to hold onto him forever.

18

EPILOGUE

Nick Firebrand should have visited his mother before now. Sitting inside his vehicle in the parking lot of county lockup, he couldn't find the willpower to remove his hands from the steering wheel or cut off the engine. The rolling gray clouds that threatened a raging thunderstorm fit his mood, dark and brooding.

He needed to get over it and force himself out of the vehicle.

Removing his Stetson to finger-comb his hair finally helped him release his grip. He muttered a curse as he glanced in the rearview. What did it matter if he was presentable or not? He was, after all, about to visit his mother in jail.

Damned if those weren't words he never thought he would mutter in a million years. And yet, there he was doing just that.

His brother Morgan's truck parked next to him. Where was Morgan's fiancée?

Nick cut his engine off and exited his vehicle. As he came around the front, Morgan met him halfway.

"Lucky coincidence?" Nick asked his brother while bringing him into a bear hug.

"Not exactly," Morgan said. "Avril saw you sitting here when we drove past a minute ago, so she figured it was a good time for me to do the same."

"Safety in numbers?" Nick half joked.

Morgan chuckled, but the tension lines around his eyes told a different story. His mouth formed a thin line. "First time?"

"Yes," Nick admitted, still not proud of the fact. He glanced over at Morgan's truck. "Where is your soon-to-be-wife, by the way?"

"She had me drop her off," he said on a shrug. "Said it might be best if I go inside to visit with you instead of her this time."

"How on earth do you explain someone like our mother to an outsider?" Nick asked, seriously bewildered. Not that he intended to have someone in his life who would require an explanation as to why his mother was in jail. The familiar anger and embarrassment he'd felt most of his life when it came to his family surfaced.

"Hey," Morgan said, interrupting his thoughts. "You okay?"

"As much as I'll ever be," Nick said on a sharp exhale. "She's our mother, so this is a no-win situation as far as I can tell. I'm here out of obligation, even though it feels like I should be here to support her. But how? How are we supposed to forget the fact she attempted murder?"

"You won't get a disagreement out of me," Morgan said before placing his hand on Nick's shoulder. "There's no rulebook for something like this. All we can do is make it up as we go and hope for the best."

Nick thought about those words.

"Have you heard Vanessa Mosely is back in town?" Morgan asked.

"No," Nick responded, stuffing down the barrage of emotions flooding him at hearing that name again. "Why would she come back to Lone Star Pass?"

"Maybe you should stop by later and ask," Morgan said, not making eye contact when he said those words.

Those should be fighting words, but Nick wasn't in the mood. "How about we deal with one catastrophe at a time?"

"A lot of time has passed," Morgan continued, not latching on to the redirect in conversation.

"Yeah?" Nick asked, but it was more statement than question. "Not enough."

With that, he turned toward the county jail and walked toward a visit he'd been avoiding. Nothing inside him wanted to see his mother in an orange prison jumpsuit or face the despair she must be feeling.

Despite her shortcomings, she was still his mother. He owed her a debt for bringing him into this world. So, he would face the music.

His brother trailed behind. Morgan seemed to realize he'd overstepped by bringing Vanessa into the conversation. Nick was serious. He could only handle one heartbreak at a time, especially the kind that made him not want to get out of bed for a solid month after a breakup that left his heart stomped on. Vanessa might as well have ground the heel of her boot in the center of his chest for the mark she'd left there.

So he was genuinely disgusted with himself for the small piece of him that wanted to know why she'd returned.

"Are you ready?" Nick asked as he reached for the door handle.

"To be honest...no," Morgan said with a tone as heavy as the clouds overhead.

Thunder cracked as the first droplets of rain fell. One splat on his forehead as he looked up to the sky.

Of all the people in the world who'd left Lone Star Pass over the years, why did Vanessa have to be the one who returned?

Keep reading to find out why Nick's ex came back to Lone Star Pass, Texas and if they'll see each other again. Click here.

ALSO BY BARB HAN

Texas Firebrand
Rancher to the Rescue
Disarming the Rancher
Rancher under Fire
Rancher on the Line
Undercover with the Rancher
Rancher in Danger
Set-Up with the Rancher
Rancher Under the Gun
Taking Cover with the Rancher

Firebrand Cowboys
VAUGHN: Firebrand Cowboys
RAFE: Firebrand Cowboys
MORGAN: Firebrand Cowboys
NICK: Firebrand Cowboys

Don't Mess With Texas Cowboys
Texas Cowboy's Protection
Texas Cowboy Justice
Texas Cowboy's Honor
Texas Cowboy Daddy
Texas Cowboy's Baby
Texas Cowboy's Bride

Texas Cowboy's Family

Texas Cowboy Sheriff

Texas Cowboy Marshal

Texas Cowboy Lawman

Texas Cowboy Officer

Texas Cowboy K9 Patrol

Cowboys of Cattle Cove

Cowboy Reckoning

Cowboy Cover-up

Cowboy Retribution

Cowboy Judgment

Cowboy Conspiracy

Cowboy Rescue

Cowboy Target

Cowboy Redemption

Cowboy Intrigue

Cowboy Ransom

For more of Barb's books, visit www.BarbHan.com.

ABOUT THE AUTHOR

Barb Han is a USA TODAY and Publisher's Weekly Bestselling Author. Reviewers have called her books "heartfelt" and "exciting."

Barb lives in Texas—her true north—with her adventurous family, and a spunky rescue who is often referred to as a hot mess. She is the proud owner of too many books (if there is such a thing). When not writing, she can be found exploring new cities, on a mountain either hiking or skiing depending on the season, or swimming in her own backyard.

Sign up for Barb's newsletter at www.BarbHan.com.

Printed in Great Britain
by Amazon